YEARNIN' FOR THE LOVE OF A THUG

BY

T. FRIDAY

Dedications

This book is dedicated to my babies: Jordin Friday, Jacob Friday, Jacory Blount, Jakayla Blount, and Jalisa Blount. Just know that everything I do and every struggle I go through, is so you guys don't have to worry about shit. Love y'all.

To my Blunt, you have been in my corner every step of the way, and I love and appreciate you for that. You have tolerated me bugging you everyday for the last 12 ½ years and never gave up on me.

To the best publisher in the world. People always say make your first choice your best choice, and I truly believe that signing my very first book contract with you was the best thing that I could have done. I appreciate you giving me a chance to write for your dope company. P.S. I also appreciate how you push me to stay on top and to keep going.

To my wonderful readers and supporters. I just really wanna say thank you from the bottom of my heart. You guys are awesome, and I appreciate you all for giving a new author a chance. I'm so happy to be some of you guys' favorite author. You all make me want to keep going strong.

To my baby sister, Amanda Jordin Hollis, there's not a day that you don't cross my mind. I swear 15 years wasn't long enough to have you here on earth with us. Love you so much my lil' white chick.

CHAPTER 1

BONES:

Bones stood outside of the prison gates. After serving a long ass five-year sentence, he was finally a free man.

"Man, where the fuck that nigga Gunna at?" He mumbled to himself.

He had reminded his right-hand man that he was getting released just the day before and now that nigga wasn't even there. Just as Bones thought he was gonna have to walk it out, a silver Denali pulled up on him.

"What's up nigga?"

Bones looked in the truck only to find his homeboys, Choppa and Gunna. "What's up my niggas? I thought you bitch ass niggas forgot about me or something."

As Bone climbed in the back seat, his homeboys laughed at him. "Nah nigga, never that. So, you ready to hit this party up and get on these hoes?" Choppa asked.

"Nigga, I just got out, what the fuck you think? I ain't trying to look at another nigga. Bring all the bitches to me," Bones replied with a laugh.

"Before we get there, let's go get you fresh right quick," Gunna said, reaching towards the back with a stack of hundred-dollar bills for his right-hand man.

"Good looking, my baby," Bone said, grabbing the money.

After bending a few more corners, they finally reached the mall. Bones walked into the mall ready to buy out some of the fucking stores. They all needed to grab some shit for Bone's welcome home party that night, so they decided to split up. The first thing Bones purchased was a phone. Being locked up for five years had him looking at some Androids before one of the workers came over to point out the latest iPhone. Bones thru them the money like it wasn't shit. He planned on getting hip to all the latest technology.

Stepping into the shoe store, he only grabbed three pair of shoes. He figured he had the rest of his life to build his gear back up to how it was before he went away. Working in the street since the age of 10, he always was the freshest young nigga around. Now that he was home, he planned on returning to his old self.

Bones stared in the store window of Urban Fashion Wear. He was feeling the whole outfit that two of the mannequins were wearing. Plus, they went good with his shoes he had just purchased. As he walked in the store, he was greeted by a friendly face and the voice of an angel.

"Hello, welcome to Urban Fashion Wear. My name is Makyla. If you need any help, please let me know."

"Makyla, before you walk off, I could use a little help," Bones said, admiring her beauty and banging as shape.

"Ok. So, what can I help you with?"

Bones gave her a little smirk. If only she knew what he was thinking.

"Everything in my closet is outdated, and I'm trying to get all the latest shit out," he explained to Makyla.

She smiled knowing she was about to make a huge sale. "No problem, follow me right over here."

Bones had no problem following her. Just watching her fat, round ass had him feeling like he would follow her anywhere.

"Ok, I personally love these jeans right here," she said, handing him a pair of jeans that looked to be torn down the leg.

He looked at the jeans strangely. "Are you fucking serious? I mean, niggas really out here wearing this shit?"

She giggled, "Yes, sir, this is the style now."

"You can stop calling me sir. I'm calling you by your name, so it's only right that you call me by mine."

"Ok, that's fair, but you never told me your name."

"My bad, shorty. My name is Brandon."

He then held his hand out, waiting to see if she was gonna shake his hand.

He was known everywhere by Bones, but for some reason, he thought that introducing himself by his government name, she wouldn't hesitate to entertain him. He was a cocky muthafucka and knew by her smile that she was feeling him.

"Ok, Brandon, here are some different type of T-shirts. We have plaid, button ups, and some with Logos on them. Which ones do you like?"

Bones smiled, "Why don't you pick out a few that you think would look good on me. Then maybe one day when I take you out, I could wear something that you picked out."

Makyla giggled, "Ok, Mr. Too Damn Smooth. I see you ain't playing no games."

Bones smiled cause no matter how she tried to play it, he knew she was feeling him. For one, since he walked in the store, she hadn't been able to stop smiling. He wasn't complaining cause her smile was beautiful. Looking over her, there wasn't shit that he could complain about.

"You laughin' at a nigga, but I'm serious. So, when we gonna go out, Makyla?" He asked.

She continued picking out a few more shirts and her smile was gone off her face. At first, he thought that she was ignoring him until he noticed her boss walking around.

"Ok, sir, will this be all or would like to look at something else?" She asked, playing everything off.

"You know what, you've done such a great job with helping me out today, I think you might need a raise."

Mr. Dickerson, Makyla's boss, heard the word raise then quickly ran off. His cheap ass wasn't trying to hear all that. Makyla was a great sales person and Bones wasn't a cheap nigga. He had purchased damn near four thousand dollars worth of clothes. He wasn't playing when he said he was trying to start his wardrobe all over. After handing him his change, she pulled out one of the stores business cards. She secretly jotted down her name and number on the back without her boss seeing her.

"Ok, sir, if you have any problems or need help with anything else, just call up the store and we'll be glad to help you out."

Bones took the card from her then made his way out the store. Just as he was walking away, he looked at the card, making sure to flip it over to the back. "I knew she was feeling me."

He soon linked back up with his boys. Their next stop was Chop's house so they could get ready for this party.

Makyla

Makyla was happy as hell to get off work. Although she needed a job to pay for her college classes, she secretly didn't care too much for her boss. She didn't understand how he was running a store for the urban community but secretly treated the customers and sometimes the employees like criminals. He allowed them to be cashiers, but when it was time to cash out a sale, he was right there watching you like a hawk. He always thought someone was gonna steal from his funky ass.

After taking a long, hot shower, Makyla stuck on some shorts and T-shirt. After work, she tried to chill and catch up on her studying and homework.

"What's up, sis?" Mike asked, walking into the front room.

"Hey, lil bro. Have you thought about what you're gonna do with yourself? I really hope you not running behind Mehki's ass."

"Damn, sis! Let me at least get in the house good before you start all that bullshit!" Mike yelled back.

He loved his big sister, but she was becoming a pain in the ass. She knew that he looked up to his big brother in a lot of ways and that scared her. Their big brother, Mehki, was a street nigga. He and his boys ran the streets and had every block on the westside on lock.

"I'm just looking out for you, lil' bro. I don't want you to end up a fucking failure like Mehki," she said, trying to sound a little calmer.

"Watch your mouth, girl," Mehki said, walking thru the front door with a duffle bag in his hand.

"Whatever boy. You need to be encouraging him to go back to school or get a job to better himself instead of being your fucking shadow. He had me help him fill out all them forms so he could attend the community college and now that school has started, he acting like that shit never happened."

"Damn, sis, you be tripping on us. Whatever I'm doing in the streets keeping the fucking bills paid. I don't see your ass talking shit in the dark!" Mehki yelled.

As crazy as it sounds, he was right. He did take care of all the bills and whatever else the house needed. "I can't wait to get the fuck away from here," Makyla said, closing her book.

"Bye," Mike said with an attitude.

He hated when they argued over him as if he was a baby. Then they talked like he wasn't even in the same room. In his mind, he was a grown ass man and could make his own decisions in life.

Makyla shook her head as she watched her brothers take a seat at the table then get to work like she wasn't standing there. Mehki started pulling out knots of money right along with his money counter. Lil Mike was all in, helping his big bro out. They sat there not paying the dirty looks that Makyla was giving them any attention. She then got up to get dress so she could leave. She hated seeing them doing that type of shit, especially when they both were smart enough to do anything else with their lives. They both had the brain power to change the world.

After getting dressed, Makyla left out the house without saying anything. She was too out done with her brothers. She took this time to drive to her home away from home. She knew her best friend, Justice, would be at home and probably cooking up some shit. At least there she could eat and do her homework in peace.

***

"What's up, girl? Why you looking all stressed out and shit?" Justice asked as she opened the door for Makyla.

Makyla walked in then jumped in the black leather recliner chair that sat in the corner of her front room.

"Bitch, these brothers of mine are getting on my fucking nerves. I know I'm not their mother, but damn, they act like they don't have no fucking sense. See, Mehki has the power to help Mike do something with his life other than be like him, but he likes the fact that Mike looks up to him."

Justice took a seat back on her black leather love seat. "Girl, I understand about you not wanting Mike to be like Mehki, but I'm really not in the right boat to complain about what Mehki do since he does take care of our son and pay all my bills. Plus, he still takes good care of me even though we're not together like that."

Makyla rolled her eyes. "I hate you fucked my brother and had a baby by him. It's so hard to vent to my best friend about my big bro when y'all are connected."

Both girls fell out into laughter.

"Whatever, bitch. I told you when we were younger that I was gonna get his sexy ass," Justice jokingly said.

Makyla pulled out her book to continue studying for her quiz that she had coming up. So stressed out about her baby brother, she could barely pay attention to what she was reading.

"Makyla, on some real shit, coming from your best friend, I think you should stop worrying about them and continue to do you. I mean, you work, and you're in your last year of college. Why come this far just to be so stressed out that you can't even focus on your work? Let them boys be boys."

Looking up at Justice, Makyla shook her head in agreement. Maybe Justice was on to something. Maybe she did need to live her life without always sitting around stressing on her grown ass brothers.

Mehki

"Man, Makyla be tripping hard over your ass," Mehki said while bagging up some of his product.

"Yeah, I see, nigga. But on some real shit, I did have her fill out my forms for school a month ago and then just said fuck it," Mike admitted.

Mehki took a pull from the kush blunt that they were passing back and forth. "Dog, don't let her ass make you feel any type of way. She might have done that shit, but it was because she wanted to. You didn't ask her to do that shit. She needs to be grateful we makin' money in this bitch 'cause that bullshit ass job ain't doing shit but putting gas in her car and feeding her on break."

Mike took the blunt from Mehki. "Yeah, nigga, you right."

The two brothers continued to bag up the work that was sitting on the table without a care in the world. The only thing on their mind was making money, stunting on niggas and flexing on these bitches.

"Anyways, bro, I'm glad to have you on my team for real now. I need a nigga to have my back, and I know I won't have shit to worry about fucking with your wild ass."

"Man, bro, don't even bring that shit up. That nigga Rell deserved that ass beating. Plus, what the fuck I look like letting that pussy nigga talk shit to me?"

"See, Mike, that's exactly why you got a higher rank in my crew. You got heart, my nigga," Mehki said, geeking his baby bro up.

Mike sat there and thought about the ass whooping he had just put on Rell. First, the nigga had been talking shit to Mike since he got serious about fucking with Mehki's crew. Then he snatched the blunt out of his hand, trying to act hard in front of the rest of the niggas on the block. Mike didn't waste no words on the nigga. He just pieced him up really quick then picked the blunt back up like it was nothing.

Rell never was a hoe or got his ass beat like that, but it was always a first time for everything. He was so embarrassed that he got up then limped away. Mehki didn't make the situation any better. He stood there testing to see if Mike was gonna boss up or bitch up. Mike did exactly what Mehki was hoping he would do. He knew he didn't help raise no bitch ass nigga.

After they were done bagging up the work that they had, Mike placed the shit in the duffle bag just how his big brother had taught him. He learned the game way before getting out of high school and couldn't wait to be just like his big brother. Although he knew it would have killed his mom if she was still alive, he knew that he needed money to survive. Most would say fast money was bad money, but he was taught from Mehki that all money spent just the same, whether you got it fast or slow.

"You want me to deliver this to that nigga Kendell?" Mike asked, picking up the bag.

Mehki chuckled, "Hell nah, nigga, you were just promoted. That's what that lil nigga James for. He on his way to get it. Plus, this the last time we touchin' this shit too. We got workers for this shit."

"Good, my nigga," Mike calmly said, taking a seat back at the table. He had a feeling that things were about to get better for him.

The brothers smoked and chilled before James came to pick up the bag. They had just invested in some new shit that was about to push them higher on the streets. If niggas didn't know who they were by now, they were about to soon find out.

Bones

"I appreciate all you niggas getting together and throwing me this party to celebrate a real nigga coming home. Y'all my niggas!" Bone yelled to a crowd of his homeboys.

Gunna and Choppa had gathered all of their people to help welcome Bones home and the turnout was great. There was plenty of food, drinks, and bitches in attendance. Most importantly, there was no drama.

Bones was in a deep conversation with a chick named Destiny when Choppa came over.

"Aye, bro, we need to talk right quick."

Bones gave Choppa a strange look. "Damn, bro, you don't see me trying to talk to this bitch?"

Destiny was heated just that quick. Turning Bones way, she began to yell, "Who the fuck you calling a bitch, nigga? You know what, fuck you hoe ass nigga!" She yelled before turning to leave.

Bones snatched her by her arm. "Bitch, you better watch your mouth before I have my cousin over there rock your shitty breath ass."

Destiny wasn't sure what girl he pointed to, but she wasn't in the mood to get her ass beat and dragged out of the party. So, to calm down the situation, she walked away without running her mouth. She felt stupid, especially since she thought that she was gonna be the first piece of pussy that he tasted since he'd been home.

Choppa was laughing hard as hell at his homeboy. His ass was always clowning a muthafucka. Low key, he was happy that Destiny wasn't about that life and did what was in her best interest. The last thing they wanted was for the club security to come over and put they ass out for fighting.

"Damn, nigga! Why you hoe that bitch like that?" Gunna asked as he joined his boys.

Bones took the blunt that Choppa was passing his way. "Fuck that hoe. She had too much fucking mouth."

After they all got another laugh at that whole Destiny situation, Choppa was the first one to get serious.

"So, Bones, you ready to get back to work tomorrow?"

Bones passed the blunt to Gunna. "My niggas, I'm all about that money shit, but give me another day. A nigga needs to be laid up in some wet, super soaker pussy before I get my hands dirty again."

"All these hoes in this bitch, pick you one, my nigga," Gunna said, encouraging his boy.

"Fuck what you talkin' 'bout, bro. I'm looking for two bad bitches. I might fuck around and kill a bitch with this back up I got. A nigga been gone too fucking long," Bones announced while pulling on the blunt.

Bones walked away to put his plan in motion. His boys were right about it being some bad bitches in the building. Many were eyeing him, ready to go fuck. At that moment, Makyla from earlier that day was running thru his mind. Bones found himself walking out of the club to give her a call.

After the fourth ring Makyla answered the phone. "Hello."

"What's up, ma? What you up to?"

"Umm, not being rude, but who is this?" Makyla said into the phone. She low key knew who it was because she didn't just have random niggas calling her phone, and she could recognize Brandon's voice. He had a certain swag about him that she liked. Right now, she was just trying to show him that he had to call her phone with some type of respect.

Trying to turn his thuggish ways down, Bones spoke into the phone. "My bad, ma. This is Brandon. I met you at your job earlier today."

Makyla was all smiles and a little surprised that he called within the first day of getting her number.

"Hey, Brandon, what's up?" She sang into the phone.

"Did I call you at a wrong time? Are you busy?" He asked.

Makyla smiled as she answered his question, "No, actually I was just finishing up some homework. What about you? What are you doing?"

Bones smiled. Usually he wouldn't sit up and hold a conversation with a bitch but there was something about Makyla that had him intrigued. He wanted to know her better.

"Homework, huh? What you in school for?" He questioned.

She smiled hard. She liked how he was actually into what she was talking about. "I'm taking up Business management. Once I'm done with this, I'm planning on running my own boutique."

"Damn, really? I like that, ma, brains and beauty. So, you design clothes and shit like that?"

"Yes, I design clothes and jewelry," she answered.

Makyla felt good talking to someone about her dreams. Her brothers never paid her any attention and probably didn't even know what she was in school for.

Feeling like she was talking too much, Makyla started asking about him. Once again, she asked, "What are you doing?"

"I'm at this club trying to live my best life, but it's lame as fuck and all these bitches busted in here."

Makyla couldn't help but to laugh. "Oh my God, you're so silly."

"Man, I'm not lying. So, what you got up?"

"I'm chilling at my best friend's house, dreading getting up early for school in the morning. Then I have to work afterwards."

"Damn, you're a busy woman. I was gonna see if you wanted to chill with me tonight, but I see it's not a good night for all that," Bones said, shaking his head. He tried to play it cool, but deep down, he really wanted to see her.

"Listen, I'm not sure what type of female you're used to talking to, but I'm not that type. I don't even know you like that, and I hope you didn't think that I was the type to give a guy my number and fuck the same night," she said with an attitude.

"Ma, you can chill on all that shit, I don't know your ass either. You actually thought I was gonna serve you this pipe on the first day of meeting you? Y'all females be tripping."

Makyla felt silly as she tried not to laugh at him, but it was so hard not to. "I'm sorry for assuming that sex was what you were looking for. You just seemed like that type-"

Before she could finish her statement, Bones cut her off. "Look, before you try to go there, let's just keep it as we both don't know each other. Truthfully, I was just trying to get to know your sexy ass. I can get pussy, that ain't never been an issue, ma. I was really trying to chill with you."

Makyla never really liked cocky niggas, but there was something about the cocky nigga Bones that was on her line.

"Ok, you're right, and maybe I was wrong for jumping to conclusions."

Seeing that he wasn't gonna get any pussy from her that night, Bones was ready to get off the phone and return to that lame ass party. "Look, how about I come get you from work tomorrow, and we can get to know each other then. How does that sound?”

"I don't know about that."

He shook his head again. This was the first time that a female gave him a challenge, but he was down for the game. "Look, I'm gonna come get you and take you out to do something. What time you get off?" He asked, basically saying fuck what she was talking about.

With a little smile on her face, Makyla gave in.

"Ok, that sounds like a plan. I get off at 3pm."

Bones had a little smirk on his face, "Ok, sexy, I'll see you tomorrow.

After hanging the phone up, Bones returned to the party. He was just gonna have to settle for one of them basic ass hoes that was in there. He didn't even make it into the door good before an old fuck buddy bumped into him.

"Damn, baby, I know you weren't trying to leave without me," Bre said as she pulled on his arm.

"Oh, you ready to slide now?" He asked, although he already knew the answer.

Bre had always been his go to pussy. Whenever he was down and out, she was always there to make him happy for the night. That was how their relationship worked. He used her then sent her ass home with a wet ass. She always wanted more, just like any other hoe, but he didn't believe in cuffing hoes. He was a street nigga and a thug. Love wasn't what he was looking for. At the age of 27, he has yet to find a bitch that could make him change his way of thinking.

Makyla

Makyla poured some orange juice while she waited for her toast to pop up. She wanted to put something on her stomach before she left for school.

"I didn't know you came home last night. Your lil' funky ass attitude gone?" Mehki asked.

Makyla wasn't trying to argue with his stupid ass before class, so she tried to ignore him. She finished making her scrambled eggs and frying her bacon as if he never said anything.

"Aye, sis, you make me something to eat?" Mike asked as he walked into the kitchen.

"No, but maybe you and Mehki can put y'all brains together and figure out how to cook your own breakfast," she coldly said.

Mike shook his head. "I see you still on that bullshit. Don't worry, I ain't gonna ask your ass for shit else."

Makyla shrugged her shoulders, letting him know that she could care less. She was giving them the funky attitude that they deserved. She hated doing Mike like that, but she had to stop babying his grown ass. As she ate her food, she watched Pinky and the Brain grab some bowls for cereal. She just laughed to herself. They were smart enough to cook dope but couldn't scramble some fucking eggs. She finished her breakfast then got ready to walk out of the door.

"See you guys later," she cheerfully said, slamming the door.

It was only a fifteen minute ride to the school, and she was happy to get a good parking spot. Her class started at 8:30am and ended at 9:45pm. It was her only class for the day, but she had to be at work from 10:30am to 3pm. That was her schedule for Tuesdays and Thursdays.

Her hour-long accounting class went by so fast; she couldn't believe it. She couldn't help but to smile as she walked out of the building and jumped in the car.

"Hey, Justice, I need you to do me a little favor," Makyla said when Justice answered after the third ring.

"What's up, boo?"

With a smile on her face, Makyla filled her friend in on her plans. "Look, I met this guy and he wants to take me out after work today. I wanna come pick you up so you can take my car."

"Wait a minute, bitch! You have some explaining to do. What nigga taking your mean ass out?" Justice asked.

Yeah, she was happy for her friend, just a little surprised that she was stepping back out on the dating scene. It had been damn near a year and a half since she had broken up with Marcus' cheating ass. Since him, she kept her heart and love to herself.

"Can you just be dressed, so I won't be late for work?" Makyla asked as she laughed at her friend and all her questions.

"Boo, I'm already dressed, but don't think I'm not gonna want some answers."

The two got off the phone and Makyla hurried to Justice's house.

CHAPTER 2

BONES

As the crew sat around the table, Bones couldn't help, but to check out all these niggas that he was gonna be working with. Well, really the way shit was set up, they were about to learn that they were gonna be working for him.

"Ok, niggas. Now that my boy Bones is back, him, Choppa and myself will be running shit," Gunna said to his team.

Hearing some of the niggas mumble or move around in their seats didn't fit well with Bones. He slowly lifted from his chair. "Do we have a fucking problem in this muthafucka? Any nigga got a problem, please come see me and we can clear it up right fucking now!" Bones yelled. The last thing that he wanted was for niggas to think he wasn't with the shits and wouldn't put a hole in a muthafucka''s head.

Choppa stood up from the table. "We all family here and I know ain't nobody tripping about positions in this bitch. Everybody eating in this bitch."

Seeing that nobody stood up to say anything, Bones sat back down with a grim look on his face. He secretly wanted a nigga to jump out of pocket so he could do them dirty. It had been a minute since he tried to tear a nigga head off.

Gunna cleared his throat. "We have the Eastside streets on lock right now and now that my bro is home, we're gonna put our hands on the Westside. This year is all about growth."

"Nigga, you ain't heard about them Westside niggas? Them boys over there running shit. They ain't 'bout to let nobody come over there and make a fucking dollar. They whole operation is flawless!" Marcus yelled out.

Bones laughed at Marcus. "Man, I hear the bitch in you, my nigga. Gunna where the fuck you recruited these soft as pussies from?"

"Who the fuck you talking to, my nigga?" Marcus asked, standing up for himself.

Bones stood up ready to go, but Gunna held his hand out, stopping him. "Bones, chill out for a minute. This nigga not familiar with you yet."

"Let's stop all the bullshit. We will be moving in soon. Fuck how their operation is being run. I'll be hitting you all up real soon with instructions and some new product. Y'all be safe out there and let's get this money," Choppa said, hoping to end all confusion and the meeting itself. The last thing Choppa wanted was for their crew to fall apart over egos. Then knowing how Bones got down, he probably would have killed Marcus before even blinking an eye.

Everyone got up from the table so they could leave. It was money to be made on the streets, and they were on their way to get it.

"Aye, bro, what you about to get into?" Gunna asked Bones as he stopped him at the door.

"I'm about to go see my ole' lady and make sure she good. Why, what's up, nigga?"

"Bro, you gotta chill out. These new niggas still learning the ropes," Gunna tried to explain.

Bones chuckled. He wasn't trying to hear that bullshit. "Fuck that shit. I was still wet behind the ears when I jumped off the porch, but I ain't bitch up to no nigga. I didn't give a fuck. These new niggas better grow some fucking balls if they wanna make money with me."

Gunna shook his head in agreement. "You right, my nigga, and that's why I'm happy to have you home. I'll holla at your wild ass later."

The two friends went their separate ways. Each had business to handle.

***

"Makyla, I'm gonna send you on your break now because Hanna called off and I need you to stay for a couple of hours."

Rolling her eyes, she instantly caught an attitude.

"I did have plans, Mr. Dickerson."

"Will, I need a cashier because Hanna called off at the last minute!" He yelled.

Makyla shook her head. "Look I have plans and you never asked me to stay. You can't just tell me I have to stay. In that case, you should have told her she had to come in and work her shift."

"Look, I'm not about to go back and forth with you. You can punch out to go on your break, or you can punch out to go home. But don't be looking for no job tomorrow!" Mr. Dickerson yelled right before walking off.

Makyla stood there in her feelings. She wanted to quit to make a point, but she needed all the money she could get for school. Plus, she was trying to save up for her own store. After thinking things thru, she clocked out for her lunch break. She just hoped Bones understood. Once she got her lunch from A&W, she hurried to grab a seat. She wasn't sure how this conversation was gonna go, but she called Bones up.

After the fourth ring, he finally picked up. "What's up, ma?"

"Hey Brandon, I kind of have some bad news," she softly said into the phone.

"Damn, don't tell me you about to flake on me and shit."

She started to explain everything to him. "My asshole for a boss just told me I had to stay for a few extra hours because a bitch called off. Then he says if I don't stay, I will no longer have a job."

"Man, are you fucking serious? Do you need me to come up there and handle his ass?" Bones asked.

She giggled, thinking he was playing, but he was dead ass serious.

"No, Brandon, I don't."

"I'm out picking up some furniture for my new crib, so why don't you call me when you get off, and I'll still come scoop you."

"Ok, that sounds like a plan. So, what do you have planned for us?" She asked.

"I wanna take you to my family little spot. I promise you're gonna enjoy yourself."

Makyla was all smiles as she listened to Brandon talk. She had been in a little bubble, trying to stay away from dating after her last heartbreak, but Brandon seemed different. She was willing to give him a chance with her.

"Ok, I'll call you once I punch out."

Bones had a smirk on his face. "Tell that muthafucka next time he pulls that shit, I'm coming up there and won't shit be pretty."

Makyla laughed, "I swear you're so silly. I'll call you later."

"Alright," Bones said before hanging up the phone.

"Damn, you already got a girl and you just came home?" April asked.

Bones turned his attention towards her. "Dang, ma! You always in my business and shit. Let's just worry about getting this furniture."

"Boy, bye. You lucky I buried that shit before your daddy found all that money. With his drinking and gambling problems, you would have come home to an empty bag. So, your business is my business."

"Damn, ma, stop tripping. You know I was just playing with your ass. But for real, she not my girl. You out of all people should know I don't believe in all that love bullshit. I'm a fucking thug," his cocky ass said with so much pride.

"What type of thug needs his mama's help to shop for furniture?" She asked, clowning him.

"Don't start with me. You already know I appreciate your taste in style."

After picking out everything for his condo, Bones was happy that they could deliver his bedroom set but pissed that the black leather couch set, and chair was gonna be delivered on a different day. Once they left the store, their next trip was Walmart. He didn't wanna be walking around the store all day, so he grabbed his personal items and a 60" TV for his room.

Bones had one more stop and that was to the dealership. He needed a new ride 'cause won't shit saying *thug* about him while riding shot gun with his ole' lady. It didn't even take him a whole five minutes to pick out his ride. Although he had his eyes on a red cutlass, he knew a nigga with his status needed a big boy ride. He quickly dropped the bread on an all red Yukon truck.

Bones was pressed with time so after driving away from the dealership, he rushed home. He knew they would be delivering his bedroom set soon. Standing in his front room looking down at the beautiful view, Bones smiled. He was fresh out of prison and could say that he was living the good life. On top of just having his freedom, he had a great position at work, a dope ass ride and a crib. The bonus was the bad ass bitch he had a date with that night.

That night, he was gonna take her to his family little spot. They hosted a dope ass comedy night on Tuesdays. He wasn't sure what type of girl she was, so this date was gonna be a test. He needed to know if she was a worth his time or if she a shack chaser. If it turned out that she wasn't shit, he was gonna fuck then call her ass an Uber.

After the guys put his room together, he paid them for the set up then sent them on their way. He pulled out his phone to see who was calling him. He smirked as he saw Makyla's name pop up.

"What's up, ma? You ready for a nigga to come get you?" He asked, hoping that she was ready and not on no bullshit.

"Yeah, I'm ready. My replacement just got here."

"Good, I'll be there in a minute. Do I need to come in or you want me to call when I get in the front so you can come right out?"

"Just call, and I'll be right out," she answered.

Bones freshened up before heading to Makyla's job. He had decided to wear one of the outfits that she had picked out just to be funny. Instead of pulling up and calling her, he did the complete opposite. Bones parked his ride then made his way to her job. He stood by the door way as she held a conversation with a co-worker.

"Makyla, you sure you don't wanna stay for these last four hours?" Janet asked.

"Hell nah, girl! I was supposed to be out of here hours ago. I'm about to enjoy the rest of my day," she said right before turning around and seeing Bones standing right there. A smile spread across her face. "Hey. How long you been waiting on me?"

"I been here for a minute, but I'm not complaining. I enjoyed watching all that ass in them tight ass pants."

Makyla laughed, "You so silly. Anyways, I'm ready to get this date started."

"Shid, me too," Bones said, checking her out again.

Once getting to his ride, he opened passenger side door for her. "I see you're a gentleman."

"Hell yeah. I do have manners," he said as he grabbed a hand full of her ass while she climbed in the truck.

She turned and gave him a dirty look.

Throwing his hands up, showing that he didn't want a problem, he quickly said, "My bad, ma, I was just trying to help you out."

Although he had a smirk on his face, she didn't go off. Now usually she would have been quick to put a nigga in his place and let them know she wasn't for all that shit, but Brandon was different. Besides being so fucking fine, his whole demeanor turned her on.

"So, where did you say we were going again?" She asked, killing the quietness between them.

"My family owns this little bar on the Eastside. It's a cool little joint. We can talk, eat, drink, dance, play pool, whatever you like. Plus, tonight is comedy night and I hear them muthafuckas be funny as hell."

Makyla smiled, "It sounds like fun, Brandon."

He smiled back at her. He liked the way she called him by his government in that sexy ass voice that she had.

They arrived in no time and grabbed a seat close enough to see the comedy show without having to worry about having to look over people's heads.

"So, what you wanna drink on?" Bones asked as he called the waitress over.

"I'm really not a drinker. so just give me a long island iced tea."

The waitress then looked over towards Bones.

"What you want nephew?"

"Auntie, you already know all a nigga fuck with is that Hennessey. And bring us some wings and fries."

He then looked over at Makyla. "Is that ok with you or you want something else?"

She turned her attention to the woman he called auntie. "Can you add on a salad with that?"

"Yes, ma'am. What type of dressing?"

"Italian will do. Thank you."

Bones watched his auntie walk off to get their food. He could tell that she was already enjoying herself just by the way she was twerking in her chair to the music.

"How about instead of twerking in that chair, you come twerk on my lap. After all, we are still waiting on our food."

Makyla blushed and for a quick second, she actually thought about taking him up on his offer. "Here come our drinks. Maybe a little later I'll dance for you."

Now he was blushing. "I'm not gonna forget either, so you better not flake on me."

After placing their drinks on the table, Bones slipped her a bill. "Keep us good tonight, auntie."

She stuffed the money in her bra. "You already know I got you. Oh yeah, y'all food coming right up."

Makyla politely said, "Thank you."

As they ate their food, they talked about whatever came to mind. It had been a minute since both of them actually went on a date, and they both were enjoying themselves. Makyla was surprised on how entertained he kept her. He was fun to be around and kept a smile on her face. Now for Bones, he was surprised that he was actually enjoying himself. He wasn't even trying to rush to get her back to his place to fuck.

He sat there listening to her explain how when she was done with school, she wanted to have enough money saved so she could buy her building for her store. Although he had heard this story before, he didn't stop her from talking. Truthfully, it was a turn on to hear a female talk about a future that didn't involve using a muthafucka for his shit. Baby girl had a real ass plan and it all involved her working hard to handle her business.

"I see you being very successful in a year or two," he added as she finished up.

"Thank you."

Makyla excused herself from the table. After drinking one and a half long island teas, she needed to go empty her bladder. While walking out the door, she watched Brandon's sexy ass just sitting there chilling. She liked the fact that he wasn't paying any of them other chicks no attention. He just sat there waiting on her to come back. She was ready to give him his dance that he asked for after telling herself in the mirror that she was gonna live her life that night.

Not paying attention to where she was going, she made a mistake and bumped into someone.

"I'm so sorry. Are you ok?" She quickly asked.

Marcus looked up to see who the clumsy bitch was. But seeing that it was his ex, he smiled. "Hey, girl, long time no see. Who you here with?"

Thinking about the way he played her, she couldn't wait to rub the fact that she was on a date in his face. "I'm actually on a date with Brandon over there," she said, pointing across the room.

"You on a date with that nigga Bones? You do know that nigga crazy and not a nigga to really fuck with like that? He a fucking killa."

"Boy, take your hating ass on somewhere," she said before coldly turning around to walk away.

Knowing that he was watching, she switched her ass before making it back to Brandon. Once there, she swaddled his lap. "Hey baby, you ready for that dance?"

"How you know that hoe ass nigga you were just talking to?" He asked.

Makyla laughed, "Man, that's my ex. We haven't been together in damn near two years. Why you ask? Do you know him?"

"I don't fuck with lame ass niggas, but I've seen him around before."

Not knowing what to say, she just nodded her head before saying, "Umm hum."

"What the fuck y'all was talking about? I saw him all in your face."

From earlier that day, he had learned that Marcus was a bitch ass nigga and wanted to know what he was running his mouth about.

"Honestly, he just said I shouldn't fuck with a nigga like you, Bones," she said, laughing.

Bones chuckled, "Yeah, that's my street name, but why the fuck he trying to throw salt on my name?"

Makyla took a sip of her drink. "It doesn't matter. I'm still here, right?"

Bone grabbed her ass cheeks before they shared a kiss. The first was just a little friendly peck, but it made him want more. He gently grabbed the back of her neck as he pulled her in for a more passionate kiss.

Finally pulling apart, she smiled at him, "So, you ready for that dance?"

"Hell yeah, ma."

Instead of a lap dance, they made their way to the dance floor. That was another reason Bones loved his people place. He could just chill and be cool without all the rap music and young dumb muthafuckas trying to start shit. The DJ had slowed it down just in time for them.

The Gap Band song, *Yearning Your Love* blasted thru the speakers.

"Wow, I haven't heard this song in so long," Makyla admitted.

"What you know about this classic?" He asked as he slow danced with her.

She giggled, "My parents used to love them and played their music all the time."

Makyla then turned around so her ass could fit perfectly on his dick. He pulled her in a little closer as he sung along with The Gap Band.

The time has come for us to stop messin' around

Cause don't you know that I like having you around in my life, oh, baby
So many times, I want to hold you, oh, so near
I want to say I love you softly in your ear
Oh, baby, don't keep running
My heart is yearning for your love
'Cause my heart is yearning for you love

Bones took his time kissing Makyla on her neck. His dick was rock hard and at that moment, he was finally ready to go fuck her. He just hoped she was into it. The way she had her ass on his dick, he couldn't help but to rub all on her body. Makyla was completely turned on by his touch. As she slowly turned around, he lifted her head up to give her another kiss.

"You ready to get up out of here?" He whispered into her ear.

Makyla wasn't the type of girl that did the *fuck on the first date* shit, but her pussy was pounding its way out her pants. She wanted him just as bad as he wanted her. She wasn't sure what to do. Her mind was telling her no because it was their first date, but her body was screaming yes.

"I don't know about all that, Brandon," she said just above a whisper.

He gave her lips a kiss again. "Look, ma. I'm not trying to pressure you into anything, but we both grown here and it's obvious that we both want each other. Be grown and come get this dick."

She couldn't help but to giggle. Although he was dead serious, he had a way to make everything funny to her. After a brief pause, she finally told him she was ready to go.

Bones signaled for his auntie to come over.

"Auntie, we about to head out." He then gave her some more money to cover their bill.

"Ok, you two be safe out there."

"Thank you. I really had a great time here tonight," Makyla said with a smile on her face.

"I'm glad you enjoyed yourself. Next time you guys should come for karaoke night."

"Ok, that sounds like a good idea," Bones agreed.

As they walked out the club, Marcus sat in the back grilling the fuck out of Bones. He hated that nigga.

Bones helped her into the car then walked over to his side. Before getting in, he told her that he would be right back. Bones walked over to a group of guys that he knew. Makyla wasn't sure what they were talking about, but at that moment, all she wanted was for him to hurry up so he could fuck her. As he started coming back for the car, she heard him tell them to call him later.

Taking his seat, Bones looked at his date. He then picked her hand up and placed it in his lap. "You ready for this, ma?"

She snatched her hand back. "Yeah, I'm ready, but are you ready for me?"

Bones laughed, "Talk that shit now, and I'll have your ass crying later."

Bones turned a couple of corners and before she knew it, they were pulling up to his condo downtown. He took her by the hand, leading her to his place. As he opened up the door, he flicked the lights on. She turned to face him with a strange look on her face.

"Look ma, I told you earlier that I was out looking for some furniture for my new place. My shit will be here tomorrow. Stop looking at me like I'm a fucking serial killa."

Realizing that he was right, Makyla smiled at him.

"My bad, baby."

"Follow me."

Makyla followed Bones down the hallway to his bedroom. She knew he wasn't about to play no games as she watched him snatch his shirt off. Once in the bedroom, Bones attacked Makyla with a kiss. She was more than ready to feel him inside of her. As they kissed, they peeled each other's clothes off one another.

He then picked her up to place her in the bed. Positioning himself in between her legs, he made his way from her full juicy lips down to her breast. He slowly took his time licking around her hard-dark nipples. Makyla moaned out in pleasure. With every touch on her body, she got wetter and moaned out for him. Bones then kissed down her stomach right before diving his face into her pretty, freshly shaven, wet pussy. As he flicked his tongue around her wetness, he made her moan out even more.

"Damn, Brandon!" She yelled out as she held on to the back of his head.

He didn't say shit as he sucked on her just a little harder. Her juices were so warm and sweet that he was ready for her to explode in his mouth.

Makyla was about to cum and couldn't help but to scream out. "Ok, baby, I'm cumming!"

Bones didn't ease up. He allowed every ounce to rush down his throat. Makyla's legs shook even after he was done. He stood next to the bed wiping his mouth off with his T-shirt. Although she was drained, she pushed herself to sit up then slid to the edge of the bed. She surprised him as she placed her mouth around his dick. She moved her head back and forth with no hands, trying her hardest to suck up every inch, and he wasn't a small nigga either. Bones had to be packing a good 11 inches and his shit was thick as hell too.

Feeling his nut build up at the tip, he pulled it out her mouth. "Turn around and throw that ass in the air," he ordered.

Makyla did as she was told. With her back arched and ass in the air, she could feel Bone's tongue right back dancing in her pussy. It felt so good that she could feel her knees trying to give out on her.

"Stop playing with me, get that ass back up here."

She managed to position herself back just the way he wanted her. Bones slapped her ass cheeks right before allowing his tongue to swirl around her butthole. Soon, his tongue had entered her, driving her crazy.

Makyla was now going crazy as he licked all the way from her ass crack back down to her pussy. Her legs started to shake again as she moaned out, "You makin' me cum again, Brandon."

Before she could release, he quickly filled her up with his rock-hard dick. Makyla couldn't even lie, she wasn't ready for that anaconda that he was carrying around. Grinding in and out of her from the back was making her go wild, and she often found herself reaching back, trying to push him back.

"It's too much, baby. Take some out," he moaned out.

"Shid, I'm not taking shit out of this warm, tight muthafucka. This shit feels too good for all that. Plus, I told you in the truck about talking all that shit. I told you that I'll have that ass crying."

Makyla couldn't stand his cocky ass at that moment. Instead of completely bitching up, she arched her back to how it was before then started throwing her ass back on him.

"That's what the fuck I'm talking about. Get that dick girl!" He yelled while slapping her ass again.

Bones ended up grabbing her hands to stop her from moving. He hated how she was trying to run again.

Makyla tried her hardest to be a big girl like he wanted her to be, but soon collapsed onto his california king sized mattress. Bones walked out to go flush the rubber down the toilet. When he returned, he found her playing like she was sleep.

"Fuck you doing? Turn yo' ass around," he ordered.

Feeling sluggish, she barely could move. He took it upon himself to flip her over.

"Oh my God! Brandon, I'm done, baby. You won," she said, laughing.

"It's not that fucking easy, girl," he said as he opened her legs back up.

He sucked on her pussy some more, causing her to get even wetter. Now that she was back soaking wet, he placed himself right back in between her legs. He said fuck a condom, he needed to feel her insides raw. He then slid his pipe right back into her. He took his time slowly stroking her pussy while keeping a tight grip around her neck. Makyla moaned out as she tried to match his pace. Between his big dick and the grip around her neck, she wasn't sure which one was gonna make her pass out first, but she loved it. The wetter she got, the more his pace sped up. Soon, he was back beating her shit up.

"Who pussy is this?" He asked.

She quickly answered, "It's yours, Brandon."

He liked her answer and continued to kill her pussy. Just as he was about to cum again, he thought about pulling out even though it felt too good. He ain't have no kids running around and didn't see no reason to start making them now.

"I'm about to cum again, Brandon!" She yelled out.

He knew the feeling. His cum was at the tip and he needed to make a quick decision. Just as he decided that the smarter thing to do was pull out, Makyla wrapped her legs around him tighter as she came.

"I'm cumming, baby."

In his mind he said fuck it then he pounded her until he finally came.

They both were tired and wore out as they laid there staring at each other. Usually this would be the time that he would ask a bitch what her plans were because he was ready for them to leave, or he would be calling her an Uber kicking her ass out. But with Makyla, he wanted her to stay. He didn't have a problem with her cuddling up on his chest before she quickly fell asleep. Bones wasn't sure what this girl was doing to him, but she had him breaking all the thug codes. It wasn't long before he was knocked out right along with her.

***

Hearing his phone ring, Bones slipped out of the bed to see who was calling him. Seeing that it was his cousin Tommy from the club, he now wore a sneaky grin.

"What's up, cuz?"

"Aye, Bones, we'll be closing soon and ole' boy still in this bitch chilling. What do you want us to do?"

It didn't even take a whole second before Bones could answer. "Quietly have everybody leave. Lock him in, and I'll be on my way."

"Ok, boss."

Their phone conversation ended just that fast.

After walking out of the bathroom, Bones gave Makyla a kiss before getting dressed. He wore all black to handle his business. Before walking out, he grabbed his gun from his shoe box in the closet. Makyla was knocked out so he knew that she would never even know that he had left.

Making it to the club in a record time, Bones hopped out of his truck. He did his secret knock before Tommy opened the door. Bones walked in to find the club empty. Besides him, Tommy and his uncle Parnell, Marcus' bitch ass was tied down to the chair and his mouth was duck taped.

Marcus saw Bones walking in pulling his hoodie off his head. He knew then that he had fucked up. He told himself that if he did make it out alive, he was gonna check Makyla about running her mouth then get the fuck on. But that was a big *if*.

Bones walked straight in, grabbing a pool stick. Marcus was now scared and started to shake his head no. Thru the tape, he begged him to let him go. Bones then whacked him across his face with the stick.

"What the fuck you were telling my girl about me?"

Whack! Whack!

"So, she shouldn't fuck with a nigga like me, huh?" Bones yelled before whacking him again.

Whack! Whack! Whack!

By the time Bones was done, Marcus' head was slumped over to the side and the floor was painted with his blood.

"Damn, nephew! You done killed the nigga before he could even answer you."

Fuck him. I really ain't wanna hear that shit anyways. "I gotta get back home to my girl before she wakes her ass up. Here, bro. Make sure you clean this shit up." Bones tossed a knot of money to his Uncle. "Split that shit with lil cuz."

After a long hot shower, Bones climbed back in the bed with Makyla. It wasn't a surprise that she was still knocked out from the dick he had just served her. Soon as she felt him back in the bed, she instantly got right back on him. Maybe he could get used to her being around.

CHAPTER 3

MIKE

Mike walked into his sister's job looking for the perfect outfit for his birthday.

"What's up Mike?" She asked.

"I need the newest shit y'all got up in here. I gotta look good for my birthday party tonight," Mike explained.

"I got you, bro. Follow me this way."

Mike followed his big sister over towards some jeans. He watched as she pulled out three pair of pants. "In my opinion, these are the sweeties and not too many niggas on to these. So, you don't have to worry about looking like the next nigga."

"Yeah, these bitches are sweet, but what shirt go with this?" He asked, looking around the store.

Makyla laughed, "I got you, bro."

Mike had noticed how her attitude was different and how she walked around the house like she was stuck in lala land. He wanted to talk to her, but working with Mehki kept him focused on the streets and it slipped his mind before.

"I see your attitude done disappeared. I can honestly say you been cool for a little over a month now. What's new, sis?"

Makyla gave her lil bro a strange look. She thought about how she should fix her mouth to tell him that for the last month or so, she had been getting the best sex in the world and a nigga done pounded her attitude away? She giggled thinking about it.

"That's because I've learned not to be so caught up in y'all bullshit and just focus on me."

Mike couldn't tell if she was telling the truth or not. So, he just shook his head, letting her know that he understood.

"Here are the shirts that goes perfect with them jeans."

Mike looked over the outfits. Even though he wasn't planning on switching up, he grabbed them all just to have them.

Makyla walked her brother to the register, so he could pay for his stuff. "Hey Kim, put this on my discount."

"Ok, no problem, girl."

After paying for his items, Mike walked towards the door. "Aye, sis, you gonna be at my party tonight, right?

"Yes, Mike. I told you soon as I get off, I'm gonna go home and get some rest. Once I get up, I'm gonna be there. I wouldn't miss it for nothing, lil bro."

"Alright, see you later," Mike said right before walking out the store.

Mr. Dickerson walked up behind Makyla. "Now that your family is gone, can you get back to work?"

Makayla rolled her eyes. "Yes, sir." She then walked away with an attitude.

It wasn't that she hated her job, but she hated her boss. He's cool when you making him money, but as soon as you look like you're actually enjoying your day, he starts bitching and shit. If she was a bitch without goals and dreams, she would have been quit working for his stupid ass.

After leaving the mall, Mike made his way to the barbershop. He didn't know why he waited until the last minute to get shit done. That had always been a bad habit of his.

Feeling his phone vibrating in his pocket, he pulled his phone out. "What's up, bro? What's good with you?"

"Happy birthday, nigga. You ready for tonight?" Mehki asked.

"Hell yeah, bro, I can't wait. I just left the shop and cracked the first bottle of the day," Mike admitted.

"Don't get too fucked up before the party. You know we're gonna have you take those 21 shots tonight," Mehki reminded him.

"Bro, I've been drinking for how long? I got this, my nigga. Anyways, I'll see your ass tonight."

Bones

"So, how that bread looking over there?" Bones asked Gunna as they counted up the money that their team made for the week.

"Shit looking good, but I still think it's about time that we expand our business to the fucking Westside and take over them streets. We would be bringing in more money."

Bones thought about what he was saying, and he was all for it. "Let's do that shit. We just need the hardest niggas on the team to open the door and soon, the rest will follow."

"Speaking of starting business West, I still haven't heard from that nigga Marcus since he bitched up a month ago," Gunna said, giving his best friend a strange look.

Bones now wore an evil smirk on his face. "Maybe the scary nigga got ghost before we could make that move. I told you that nigga was a bitch."

Gunna shook his head. He knew his boy all too well and wasn't buying that bullshit.

"Yeah ok, nigga. We can stick to that story," Gunna said, now laughing.

"Damn, what time is it?" Bones asked, pulling out his phone. He noticed that it was just about time for Makyla to get off. He wanted to call her before she went home and made plans for the rest of the night.

"Since shit looking good here, I'm gonna head out."

Before Bones could walk out the door, Gunna called out for him. "Bones! Look, bro, be careful out here and try to stay out of trouble."

"For sure, my nigga," Bones said before leaving out.

Hopping in his truck, Bones pulled out his phone. He wanted to catch Makyla before she went home and made plans for the rest of the day. It was weird how besides making money, she was always on his mind. She was doing something to him, and it was more than that fat ass and good pussy she was carrying around.

"Hey, baby," she cheerfully answered on the third ring.

"What's up, ma? What the fuck you got up for the rest of the day? You trying to slide thru and fuck with a nigga?"

"Damn, baby. That sounds good, but I told you that today was my lil' brother's birthday and his party is tonight. I asked you if you wanted to go with me. Do you remember?"

Bones was somewhat disappointed. He had become so used to her being around him when he wasn't in the streets. He had to admit that she wasn't like any other female that he had dealt with in the past. He wasn't going soft or nothing, and he still stood his ground on not believing in that love bullshit. He was a fucking thug, he was just having fun. Will, that's what he told himself everyday.

"Yeah, I remember now. I might slide thru and kick it with you a lil later."

"Ok, Brandon," she said, rolling her eyes. She really wanted him to hang with her that night.

Bones shook his head. He knew that she hated not getting her way and had an attitude.

"Makyla, I'm about to go see my Ole' G and see what's up with her. I'll call you in a few and let you know what's up."

"Ok, baby," she said a little more cheerful. She now had high hopes that he would show up.

After getting off the phone, Bones made his way to his mom's house. He wanted to drop her off some money and make sure she was straight. Pulling up, he saw that she was chilling on the porch drinking some iced tea.

"Hey, ma," he said, giving her a kiss on the cheek.

She quickly whipped her face. "Boy, have you lost your fucking mind? Don't be putting your nasty mouth on me. I don't know where it's been!" She yelled out, acting all dramatic and shit.

Bones laughed before taking a seat next to her. "My bad, ma. You right I been wildin' out, eating pussy and ass nonstop for a month straight from a bad bitch," he said, now laughing at the disgusting face she was making. "Nasty ass muthafucka. Your lips gonna fall off
your fucking face."

Bones continued to laugh and fuck with his mama.

"Shid, it's so fucking wet and juicy, it might be all worthit."

April hit her son in his chest before getting up to go in the house. She was so disgusted by his words, and he thought it was so fucking funny. Knowing that he had pissed her off, he got up to check on her. As he walked in the house, he went into the kitchen. The smell of food cooking filled his nostrils. He saw his mom sitting at the island.

"Ma, you done got too fucking sensitive. You know I was just playing with your ass," he tried to explain.

"I ain't nowhere near soft, but you just get on my fucking nerves sometimes."

"Sorry, ma."

"So, when can I meet this lil bitch who got you wide open?" She finally asked.

Bones gave his mama a strange look. "You got me fucked up. Ain't no bitch got me wide open. If anything, I'm the thug busting them wide open."

"Whatever, I know you. You're my son and I can tell that this ain't just a regular fuck buddy. I wanna meet her so I can see my future daughter-in-law. Plus, it's time for me to have some grandbabies."

Bones picked up her glass then took a sip.

"What the fuck you are doing boy?" She yelled.

"Trying to see what the fuck your ass over there drinking on. You got to be fucked up talking about me having kids and shit. I can't be no thug with kids running around. And I damn sure ain't fucked a bitch worthy of having my seed."

April shook her head. "You sound so dumb. You are your father's child, a fucking retard."

Bones stood up before digging in his pocket. "Here, take this money. I'll give you that before I give you a damn grand baby."

April took the money from out his hand and didn't say anything else. He knew exactly how to make her shut up.

"Alright, ma, I'm about to head out. I had enough of your crazy ass for the day."

They both started to laugh.

"I'm not asking for much, Bones. At least let me meet the girl, so I can have some type of hope. I don't care what you say, she different from the rest."

Bones stood there for a minute before telling her,

"I'll think about it, Ma, but I'm not promising you shit."

"I'll take that, I guess," April said before walking her son out the door.

As he drove off, she sat back down in her chair to finish her drink. She knew whatever girl he had been dealing with had him wide open. She could recall him buying roses and shit for the girl. He had finally met his match and deep down inside, she knew it.

Later that night

"Shot, shot, shot!" Everyone yelled as Mike took his 21 shots of Hennessey.

He tried his best not to fumble, but after shot seven, he felt that shit creeping up on him.

"That's why I told your hardheaded ass not to drink earlier. Now you about to be fucked up!" Mehki yelled over the music.

"I'm good, bro. Plus, my big sis gon' help me out."

Makyla laughed, "No, I'm not. Mike, you on your own. Besides, I have to work tomorrow."

Mike's homeboy, Ron, stood up from the booth.

"Why don't I get a picture of y'all all together taking a shot?"

They turned towards Makyla to see if she was down.

"Fuck all that shit, sis. It's my muthafucking birthday, you better come drink with me," Mike order.

He then handed her a shot glass. They all took a shot for Mike's birthday while Ron took the picture. Everyone was good after their drink but Makyla's crazy ass. After her first shot, she necked another one. From there, she started singing and dancing. Her brothers were just glad she was having a good time.

Mehki shook his head as she got loud. "Back, back-backin' it up, I'm the queen of talking shit then I'm backin it up."

"Aye, nigga, stop looking at my fucking sister!" Mehki yelled at Ron.

"Nigga, you sound crazy. She backin' that ass up. You'll think something wrong with me for not looking," Ron said, laughing.

"It's bro birthday and we are having a good time, so I'll let that shit pass," Mehki said, shaking his head at their friend.

They all continued to celebrate Mike's 21st birthday. Everyone was having a good time and all the drama was left outside of the building.

"Ok y'all. I'm done for the night. I'm about to call it a night," Makyla announced after a few more drinks.

Mehki walked her out to her car after she hugged almost everyone. "I'm glad you loosened up and enjoyed yourself."

"Yeah, I did have a good time. I actually missed hanging with y'all two. Maybe we all should start doing more shit together."

"We are sis. We all we got and have to remember that shit," he said, helping her into the car.

"Y'all be good and don't be out all night."

Mehki laughed, "Yes, ma'am. You be safe going home. I'll have bro home in a few."

Makyla drove off. She was buzzing a little but made it home safe. After finally making it home, she took a hot shower before slipping on a T-shirt and a pair of red laced panties. Soon as her head hit the pillow, she was knocked out.

Mike & Mehki

Mike had just walked out of the restroom when he bumped into that nigga Rell.

"Excuse you, nigga," Rell said, trying to act hard.

"Boy, fuck you. How about that, bitch?" Mike barked.

He hated that nigga Rell and it was crazy 'cause it was all over a bitch.

"Suck my dick, nigga!" Rell barked back.

Mike was ready to fight, but instead, he laughed then walked away. He tried to return to his party and be cool, but he was heated and wanted to put a hole in a nigga head.

"Bro, I'm about to fuck that nigga Rell up if he keeps looking over here," Mike told his brother.

Mehki was fucked up and didn't care about keeping the peace. Since Mike and Rell had got in that fight a while ago, Rell stopped working for them anyway. Mehki couldn't save his ass any more. It was all fair game now. He was hoping Rell wasn't begging for another ass whipping 'cause his bro was gonna deliver it. Mike sat there grilling Rell. Rell wasn't a hoe about the shit either. He had his boys with him, and they all were ready for the green light.

"So, what? You niggas just gon' stare at each other from across the room and blow kisses. If you don't go handle that shit, bro," Mehki said, egging his little brother on.

Mike stood up and his boys followed. Rell was hip to the game, so him and his crew stood up, but instead of approaching Mike, they walked outside. They weren't running from the fight, they were ready to rumble.

"Let's go!" Ron yelled out.

Mike hurried outside. He was ready to put Rell on his head again. Without giving Rell a chance to say a word, Mike came straight out swinging, dropping them blows at his weak ass. Them fighting caused everyone to start fighting in the parking lot, and there wasn't shit the security guards could do. Just as shit was getting good, someone in the crowd started busting shots. That caused everyone to scatter and go crazy. Rell and his people took off one way while Mike and Mehki jumped in the car. Mehki was happy that his brother left his car at home and rode with him.

They quickly drove away from the club but slowed down a few blocks away seeing the police on their way towards the club. They didn't want no unnecessary problems on their hands.

"I'm proud of you, nigga. You handle your shit and beat that nigga ass again. But you know this little beef between y'all ain't gon' never end, bro. You might have to take that nigga out."

Mike was still heated and quickly yelled out, "That ain't shit! Roll up to that nigga crib!"

Mehki chuckled, "Bro, you ready to place that body under your belt?"

"Been ready, my nigga."

Mehki busted a couple of turns before pulling up on an empty street in Highland Park. He killed his engine then lit his blunt.

"That nigga mama lives over there. We can wait and catch that nigga pulling up," Mehki suggested.

"That nigga just got his ass beat. Trust me, he ain't coming home tonight. I bet if you ride pass that nigga Jay house, he over there talking mad shit."

Mehki started his car back up. "You might be on to something."

The brothers drove in silence. Mike was low key nervous. He had never killed a nigga before, but he knew it was time to put in that work. If he allowed Rell to live a day longer, that nigga would have taken him out first. At the end of the day, it was his life over that nigga's life.

Approaching Jay's block, Mehki killed his lights. He slowly drove up the block checking out the scenario. Just like lil bro said, Rell, Jay, and a nigga name Deandre were standing in front of Jay's house smoking and running their mouth like a bunch of bitches.

"How you wanna handle this, bro? Hit them all or just Rell?"

Mike wasn't himself that night and when he opened the door without answering the question, Mehki knew that he had helped create a fucking monster. Mike didn't even shut his door as he snuck up on them niggas busting. Mehki was right behind him. Mike's bullets were only hitting Rell, but Mehki handled the other two niggas. He made sure he hit them before they had a chance to pull out their gun and retaliate.

Once all three of their bodies were stretched out on the grass, Mehki grabbed Mike.

"Come on nigga, let's get the fuck on."

Just as he was starting to jog to the car, he turned around to check on his brother but saw him now standing over Rell's body. Soon as he was about to yell and tell him to bring his ass on, Mike let off two more shots in that nigga head. That's when Mike ran back to the car.

The drive home was silent. Neither brother knew what to say to each other at that time. Mehki wanted to just get the lil nigga home so he could get some rest.

Makyla

Makyla's sleep was interrupted by the sounds of screaming and crying. She jumped up realizing that it was both of her brothers. Not knowing what she was walking into, she slowly followed the sounds.

"Mike, you good, bro. You got to chill the fuck out now!" Mike yelled.

Makyla then heard Mike crying out something, but she couldn't make out what he was saying.

"What the fuck is going on here?" She yelled from the bathroom doorway.

"Makyla, get the fuck in your room!" Mehki yelled.

She looked at Mike as he vomited into the toilet. At first, she thought that he had gotten drunk until he stood up. She then noticed the blood on his white shirt.

"What the fuck did y'all do?" She yelled out as she began to cry. Deep down inside, she knew the truth.

"Get the fuck on please. He's gonna be alright, he just need to get some rest. Every nigga falls apart after catching their first body," Mehki said.

Mike stood there for a minute before leaning back down to vomit some more. For a split second, Makyla lost her mind and started attacking Mehki. Deep down in her heart, she knew whatever Mike did, he was responsible. Oh my God!

She swung her fist at him all while yelling. "What did you make him do, Mehki? Who did y'all hurt?"

Mehki tried blocking her fist, but eventually bossed up. He quickly grabbed her hands right before tossing her ass onto the hallway closet door. "Get the fuck away from me, bitch."

Soon as the bitch word left his mouth, he wanted to take it back. She instantly started to cry. He had never disrespected her like that, and it hurt her deeply. Makyla then hurried to her room, slamming the door. Knowing that he had fucked up, Mehki went into the living room. He took a seat on the couch trying to calm down.

Makyla pulled out her overnight bag and quickly thru some clothes into it. She then grabbed her hygiene products, placing them into the bag. She had a plan to go to Justice's house. As she was walking pass Mehki on the couch, he reached out and grab her.

"Sis, I'm sorry, man. You know you're my fucking heart and I didn't mean that shit."

Makyla didn't wanna hear all that shit. She snatched her hand back. "Fuck you, Mehki. You ain't shit and you done pulled Mike into your bullshit. You fucked up his life."

He was hurt and didn't know what to say after that. He sat back on the couch and let her walk out the door. Yeah, it was almost 3am, but he knew she wasn't going nowhere but to his baby mama house.

Sitting in her car, she continued to cry. Never had she felt so disrespected, especially by her brother. As she thought about everything, she knew she couldn't go to Justice's house. It was 3am and she knew her brother would be at her house first thing in the morning trying to get her to come back home. Or worse, he would have talked Justice into begging her to forgive him.

She then pulled out her phone, dialing the only person number who she probably could count on right now.

Bones sat up to grab his phone. He wasn't sure who the fuck was calling him that late, but he was about to go off. What pissed him off more is that by the time he got to the phone, whoever it was had hung up. He unlocked his phone to see who it was. He looked at the screen only to see that Makyla had called him. Thinking that she had just left the club and probably was drunk looking for some dick, he hurried to call her back.

Since he didn't answer the first time, Makyla didn't know what she was gonna do at first. She thought about just spending some of her savings to get a room. There was no way she was gonna stay in that house with them two fools. Hearing her phone ring took her out of her thoughts. Although she was crying, she still managed to smile a little.

"Hello," she softly said into the phone.

Right from jump, Bones could tell that something was wrong, and she had been crying.

"What's up, ma? You good?"

Crying harder now, she began to talk, "I'm sorry for calling so late. I just didn't know who else I could turn to."

"Makyla, what's going on? Where you at so I can come get you?"

Hearing her cry did something to him. At this point, he was sliding on some sweat pants and shoes.

"Where you at?" He asked again, grabbing his gun from out his drawer. He wasn't sure about what was going on, but he was ready to put a whole in a muthafucka for pissing her off.

Makyla calmed down long enough to talk.

"Brandon, can I come over?"

"You know you ain't never gotta ask that shit. Come on."

Makyla said Thank you, right before hanging up.

***

Soon as Bones opened the door for Makyla, she fell into his arms crying. He held on to her for a few minutes before pulling her into the house.

"Come on ma, pull yourself together and tell me what happened," Bones said, leading her over to the couch.

Makyla really didn't wanna tell him everything that happened that night. She really just wanted him to hold her and tell her that everything was gonna be alright.

As he laid down, she placed her body right on top of his. He slowly rubbed her back, trying to make her calm down.

"Who did it?" He asked.

"Baby, I don't wanna talk about it. I just can't be in that house anymore," she softly cried out.

Bones remembered her telling him that she lived with her family, so he didn't take it personal that she didn't want to talk about it. He then placed a kiss on her forehead. "It's gonna be alright, ma."

The couple held on to each other and soon, the body heat between them put them straight to sleep right on the couch.

Hearing her phone go off back to back woke Bones up from his sleep. "Makyla, somebody keep calling you. Get up and get your phone."

"No, let it ring. I already know who it is," she mumbled, still halfway sleep.

"Get your ass up and put that bitch on silent or something," Bones ordered. He too was still half ass sleep and annoyed by the phone.

Makyla got off his chest to put the phone on silent. She then started walking towards the back of the house. She was ready to get in the bed. Bones got up to follow her sexy ass to the bedroom. Watching her ass made him hard as a rock, and he was ready to fuck away all her problems. Stepping out his sweatpants, Bones watched as Makyla took off her leggings and then her t- shirt. She was only wearing a pair of lace panties. Bones cuffed his dick.

"You might as will take those muthafucka off too. You know I don't allow clothes in my fucking bed."

Makyla giggled while pulling her panties off.

"You so silly, baby. Now come put me back to sleep."

Bones was never good with following orders, but when it came to her sexy ass, he was on his best behavior. In no time, they were in the bed fucking like wild animals. By the time the sun was coming up, he was feeling her up with his cum.

Before he pulled out, Bones gave her a kiss on her forehead. Makayla did the same thing she did each time she slept with him. She cuddled up right on his chest.

"You feel a little better?" He asked.

"Yeah. Well, for now, I guess. Some shit popped off at my house and to be honest, I really don't wanna go back there and deal with the shit."

"You gotta work or go to school tomorrow?"

"I have to work six hours tomorrow. Why, what you have in mind?"

"Nothing really," he lied. Truthfully, he wanted her to ride with him to his mom's house so she could get off his back.

He then gave her another kiss. "Get some rest, baby."

Makyla rubbed her hands over his tattooed chest.

"Baby, I love you."

CHAPTER 4

MAKYLA & BONES

Bones slipped out of the bed trying not to wake Makyla up, knowing he was gonna have to deal with the shit that happened before they went to bed but didn't know how. They fucked until the sun came up, then she fucked around and used those three words that scared him. How was he gonna keep her around if he didn't really believe in all that love shit? Thugs didn't do that type of shit in his book. After handling his business, Bones went into the living room to roll up his breakfast. He needed to get his thoughts in order before she got out of the bed.

Makyla jumped straight out of the bed and went into the bathroom. She was feeling a little stupid and was ready to leave. She wasn't sure how she was gonna face him after making a fool of herself. All while in the shower, she replayed how she was a fool by telling Bones that she loved him, only for him to play sleep like they weren't just in the middle of a conversation. Makyla's mind was all over the place as she thought that she had made it too easy for him to get to her. She allowed him to break the wall down that she had around her heart and now she wasn't sure if he ever really wanted it.

Just as she was stepping out the shower and wrapping her towel around her wet body, Bones walked into the bathroom.

"Damn, you won't gon' wait for me?" He asked.

"Nah, I'm actually in a hurry and need to be headed out."

Bones could sense the attitude in her voice but wasn't sure how to fix it. What was he supposed to say? Thank you for loving a thug nigga like me?

Bones stood in the doorway, blocking her from walking way. "I thought you didn't have to work until this afternoon. What's the rush for?"

"Excuse me, I would like to go get dressed and you're in my way," she said.

Bones moved to the side so she could walk pass. As he followed her into the room, he grabbed her from behind. She tried to get away but couldn't.

"Brandon, stop playing with me. I told you I had to get dressed!" She yelled, trying not to laugh at him.

"Fuck all that. You walkin' around with a fucked-up attitude, and I'm not feeling it."

"Well, how the fuck I'm supposed to act after feeling like a fool?"

Bones took a seat on the bed. He watched as she started to get dressed. "Why do you feel like a fool, Makyla?"

She smacked her lips. "Why do you think? I told you how I felt, and you completely ignored my feelings. So, yeah, I feel like a fool and just need to leave."

Bones shook his head. "Look ma, don't feel foolish for loving me. I'm a lovable nigga and shit like that happens."

"Fuck you."

Bones stood up from the bed. She said some shit that he didn't like, and she was only seconds away from meeting the real Bones.

"What the fuck you say?" He firmly said, walking closer towards her.

She looked up at him but could tell that she had pissed him off. Makyla had enough sense not to repeat herself. He stood right over her with a grim look on his face. He hated bitches with smart ass mouths and usually would have been knocked her fucking head off but looking into her eyes stopped him from acting up.

"What the fuck you say? I don't think I heard you right. Repeat that shit for me."

Not being stupid, she walked away towards the nightstand where her ringing phone was at. She looked at the screen and was happy that it wasn't Mehki or Mike's ass calling her again.

"Hello," she calmly said into the phone.

Bones stood there listening to her conversation. He wasn't sure who it was, but they had pissed her off even more. She had even started yelling saying that whatever happened was some bullshit. By the time she got off the phone, it looked like she wanted to cry. She must have gotten in trouble at work because Bones heard her tell whoever it was that she needed all her hours so she could pay for school.

Soon as she got off the phone, Bones went over to her. He placed a kiss on her lips before asking if she was ok.

"What's good, ma? You good?"

Forgetting that she was just seconds away from getting her head knocked off, she allowed him to hug her.

"So, yesterday I let my lil' brother use my discount for his birthday outfit and my stupid ass boss didn't say anythingwhen it happened. He let me continue to work the whole day, but today he called talking about I'm suspended for two weeks. I swear I hate that man."

"I know you not about to cry over that shit?"

"Man, you just don't understand, Brandon. I need to work so I can pay for my classes. Plus, how I'm supposed to be saving for my business if I can't work? Then, I told you I needed to move. He really just fucked me over with this shit," she explained.

Bones understood her grind and actually liked it. Most bitches weren't thinking about their future. That was one of the reasons he kept her around.

"Look, don't worry about that shit. You're gonna be good."

Makyla pulled back from him. "I need to just get dressed, go get my laptop and go job hunting."

"Look, I understand your grind, ma, but don't stress over that shit. You're too beautiful to be walking around letting that bitch ass nigga stress you out."

Bones pulled her back in his arms. She tried not to be so caught up in him, but it was so hard as he placed small kisses on her lips then her neck. He was trying to be so slick as he rubbed all over her booty. It wasn't long before his hands were pulling her panties down.

"I'm not about to be playing with you, Brandon," she said, stepping back and pulling her panties back up.

"You really about to leave me like this, man?"

Makyla looked down and could see that he was rock hard. She giggled knowing that he wasn't about to let her leave while he was like that. She had to just deal with the fact that she was in love with a thug, and he wasn't feeling the same yet.

Before she knew it, she had her face down on the mattress with her ass tooted up in the air. Bones was in his favorite position, tongue sliding up and down from her ass to her pussy. The way he made her cum back to back, Makyla felt deep down inside that he really did have feelings for her and was just scared to show them.

Makyla had just came for the second time when her body collapsed on the bed. "Damn, baby."

"Yeah, yeah, I know. I'm a pro at what I do."

"Cocky ass muthafucka."

Bones positioned himself in between her legs.\

"You love my cocky ass doe."

She fixed her mouth to say some smart shit but couldn't even get it out. Bones knew she was about to start talking shit, so he filled her up with eleven inches of rock-hard dick. He started off slow but seeing how she was trying to match his pace, he quickly picked up speed. He laughed seeing that her ass was no longer trying to act like she was on his level.

"What's that shit your lil ass be talking? You actin' like I don't be tearing this shit up every single time."

Makyla couldn't say shit as he pounded away with her legs up in the air. It wasn't long before she was begging him to slow down.

"Baby, slow down a little, or at least put my legs down."

"Fuck that shit. I'm keeping you just like this until I cum. I ain't forgot about that shit you said earlier."

He wasn't playing with her as he went to work.

"Fuck, baby. Ok, you win, I quit," she moaned out.

He laughed but kept going. He soon felt his nut at the tip and was ready to fill her up. Looking down at her face showed him that she had enough.

"You lucky," was all he said before letting her legs down, then releasing in her. His body soon after dropped on top of hers.

"Get your big ass off me, nigga."

"Shut your smart mouth ass up before I go back up in that pussy."

Makyla didn't say shit. She cuddled on her boo just like any other time.

"I'm kind of glad you don't have to work today. Now I can take you somewhere. I want you to meet somebody."

"Who?" She asked.

"You'll see later. Let's just go back to sleep for now. It's gonna be a long day."

Mehki & Justice

"That's your so-called best friend and you sitting up here telling me you don't know where the fuck she at!" Mehki yelled at Justice.

"You the one who put your hands on her and called her a bitch. How the fuck you mad 'cause you fucked up and now she don't wanna be bothered with your ass!" Justice yelled back.

"I know I fucked up, but I would have thought she would have brought her stubborn ass over here. Where the fuck she at, Justice?"

Justice watched as her baby daddy took a seat next to her, "Mehki, I swear, baby. I don't know where she at. For a matter of fact, I haven't even talked to her today. You want me to call her for you?"

"Yeah, do that 'cause her ass ain't answering for me or bro. That nigga at home locked in his room going crazy."

Justice pulled out her phone to call her bestie. She allowed the phone to ring until Makyla's voicemail came on. "I guess she's not answering for me either."

"I hate this shit, man. She gon' make me pull up on her at work," Mehki said, very upset.

Justice didn't respond. She was wondering why her so-called best friend would ignore her calls just because she was mad at her brother. She never knew what the fuck could have been going on with her.

"Lil man sleep?" Mehki suddenly asked.

"Yeah, he knocked out. Don't you remember me telling you that he wasn't feeling good? He had some soup and orange juice for breakfast. After eating then taking his medicine, he laid down and watched TV until he fell asleep," Justice explained.

With a smirk on his face, Mehki started to rub on Justice's thick thighs. "Let's go in the room right quick."

Justice wasn't falling for his shit. She pushed his hand off her. "I'm good, Mehki. Why don't you go call one of those hoes that be chilling in the trap with your ass?"

"Why the fuck every time I come over here and try to get some pussy, you talking shit? Why you can't just make sure your baby daddy good?" He asked.

"I told you that I wasn't into letting a nigga play me or fuck with my feelings. You wanna pop up over here and play house, but don't wanna make no fucking commitment."

"Fuck all that, we have a baby together. What the fuck we really need titles for?" Mehki asked, raising his voice.

Justice rolled her eyes. "Because, Mehki, you not about to string me along. One minute you wanna act like you love me and you wanna be a family man, but then you switch everything around and wanna be out in the streets doing whatever you wanna do."

"I'm just saying, Justice, you're my baby mama. I should be able to fuck whenever I want to. Ain't being my baby mama a good enough title? No other bitch got that title but you."

Justice was now softly crying. It was hard loving a nigga who just didn't understand what love was. She was deeply in love with Mehki, but he was just so street sometimes, and he refused to settle down.

"Just leave, Mehki. I don't wanna do this shit with you anymore," she cried out.

"Man, I don't know why you all in your feelings and shit. You know I love your cry baby ass. Don't I take good care of you and Lil man?"

"Yeah, you take good care of us with designer and flashy shit. But what about my heart? I'm not understanding why we just can't be together and be a family. Why is it so hard for you to commit to me?" She cried out.

Mehki shook his head. He didn't understand why she was tripping. They were never really together in the first place. She was just always around the house and one day he pulled her into his bedroom to chill with him. Next thing he knew, she was always coming around to get fucked. Then one day, she popped up pregnant. A relationship was something that they were never in, and he had a feeling that she only wanted one 'cause his name rang bills out in the streets and hoes was always on his dick. She couldn't handle just being his baby mama anymore.

Not wanting to argue with her anymore, Mehki stood up from the couch, dug in his pocket, then pulled out some cash. Justice watched as he placed a stack on the coffee table. "Here, this should be good for a minute. I'm about to head back to the crib."

Hating that he was about to leave, she jumped up from the couch. "Wait, Mehki. Look, baby. I don't care about that money. It's always been about you. I love you, Mehki."

Mehki wrapped her up in his arms. He then placed a kiss on her lips. "You know I love you too.

As they shared a passionate kiss and he started to pull at her clothes, Justice prayed that she wasn't making a mistake, and he now wanted what she wanted. Without say6ing a word, Mehki picked Justice up and carried her into the bedroom. He loved his baby mama and was gonna try to make her happy. He'll be damned if he fucked up and let another nigga be around his son.

Mehki positioned himself between her legs and was met by her wetness. As he slid in her goodies, he couldn't help but to love how his dick fit perfectly inside her walls. The way they fit perfectly with each other let him know that he still was the only one who had been inside of her. The couple made love and constantly allowed the words *I love you* flow out of their mouths. It wasn't long before they both came together.

As she rested her head on his chest, Justice rubbed his chest while he rubbed his hands thru her hair. This was something that they always did after making love.

"I love you, Mehki," she whispered.

"I love you too, girl, but you should already know that."

"I know, baby and I'm sorry for always tripping on you. I just don't wanna lose you to one of those hoes that only want you for your money when I for sure want you for your heart."

Mehki looked down at his baby mama. He understood where she was coming from, but at the same time, he wanted her to understand that no matter what, she would always have him and his heart.

"I love you too, Justice. You don't have to worry about shit, you got me, ma."

He then placed a kiss on her forehead right before they both dozed off.

Justice ended up waking up to the sound of her son knocking on the door. After getting dressed, she opened the door for her five-year-old son. He looked identical to his dad as he stood there smiling.

"Mommy, can I have some juice?" Mehki Jr., asked.

"Yeah, come on, let's go to the kitchen," Justice said, leading him into their kitchen.

Mekhi Jr. took a seat at the table while waiting on his juice. "Mommy, I'm hungry too. I don't want no more soup."

"Ok then, lil boy. What do you want to eat then?" She asked.

"I want my daddy to cook. Can I go wake him up?"

Justice giggled. She knew that her son was a true daddy's boy and just wanted to see his daddy. Lil Man thought he was slick.

"How about you go find something for us to watch on TV, and I'll go get him for you. Does that sound like a plan?"

Mehki Jr. cheerfully jumped up from his seat.

"Yes, mommy, go get him."

Justice walked in the room just in time to see Mehki putting his pants back on. "Hey baby, I'm about to cook and Lil Man is in the living room waiting for you."

"Man, I can't chill today. Mike all fucked up, so I have to go handle some business. I'll be back tomorrow or something."

Justice was pissed now. "I'm so sick of the streets coming before us, Mehki. You go out there and explain to your son how the streets are more important than spending time with him!" She yelled.

"That's not what the fuck I said, so chill the fuck out with that bullshit. You know I love my son, but I can't take care of him without making money!" He yelled back.

"Fuck you, Mehki. Go ahead and take your sorry ass on somewhere."

Before she knew what happened, Mehki had her pinned up on the wall by her neck.

"How the fuck you gonna say fuck me? I'll fuck your ass up if you ever say that shit again. Bitch, you got me fucked up."

"Daddy, don't fight mommy!" Mehki Jr. yelled, standing in the doorway.

What was going on in that room was something that Mehki nor Justice ever wanted their son to witness. Mehki slowly let go of Justice's neck. She stood there crying as he walked out with their son.

It was crazy how one minute they were expressin their feelings, telling each other how much they loved one another, then the next minute, he was calling her a bitch and choking her up. She cried as she told herself that this wasn't the type of love that she wanted.

Mehki felt bad, but only because this time his son had walked in on their shit. He tried so hard not to be the type of nigga that had to put his hands on a female, especially the woman that had blessed him with a child, but sometimes her mouth was so fucking reckless. He did everything for her, and she fixed her mouth to say fuck him.

Mehki called James and told him that he was caught up in something, so he'll have to handle whatever was going on. He then started cooking the hamburger meat for his son's tacos. As he went into the living room, he could tell that his son was pissed off at what he saw, so he tried to make things right with him.

"Aye, you know daddy sorry for putting his hands-on mommy. I'm not gonna do that shit again, I promise."

Lil Man smiled. "It's ok, Daddy, just make sure you tell Mommy the same thing, so she won't be mad at you."

"I am, son, I am."

They sat on the couch eating tacos and watching cartoons. Mehki had to admit that spending time with his son was better than running the streets any day. He needed to get his shit together and real soon.

Makyla & Bones

"Baby, are you gonna tell me where were going?" Makyla asked as she put on her lip gloss.

"I told you it was a surprise. Now put your seatbelt on so we can be on our way," Bones ordered.

She did as she was told. While they drove in silence, she strolled thru Facebook. Although she didn't hang around a lot of people, she had so many so-called friends online. While stopping at a red light, she moved in closer towards Bones before snapping a picture.

"We look good together."

"Yeah, we do, but don't put that online."

"It's too late, baby. It's already saved as my profile picture. What's the problem?"

"It really ain't a problem, I just don't do that Fakebook shit. Muthafuckas just be lurking on people pages to be nosey and shit."

"So, do you really want me to delete it then?" She asked, hoping he wouldn't say yeah.

"You know what, go ahead and keep it. I like that picture of us anyways," he said with a smile.

He wasn't sure what she was doing to him, but he never was ointo bitches posting his picture online. To him, that was a way of bragging to other bitches that she finally got dicked down by him. Soon as Makyla started to put her phone in her fanny pack, her notifications started to go off. As she looked at what was going on, she started to laugh.

"What's so funny, ma?"

"Everybody on here asking me who you are. Oh, my gawd! This dumb ass just tagged my brothers trying to start some shit. I hate messy muthafuckas," she said as she blocked the person who tagged Mehki and Mike.

"That's exactly why I don't do that social media shit. I'll fuck around and crack a nigga skull," Bones said, pulling up to a jewelry store.

"I think I'm just gonna erase it, baby. I'll just keep it in my phone."

Bones didn't care. Either way, he knew nobody better not had come to him on no fuck shit or it was gonna be lights out for them.

Finally putting her phone away, Makyla looked up at their location. "Baby, what we doing here?"

"Come on, just get your ass out."

Although he was dead as serious, she laughed. "You a goofy ass muthafucka."

Makyla continued to laugh before saying,

"Whatever boy."

As they walked around the store, Makyla spotted a bracelet that she liked but knew at that moment she couldn't afford to make a purchase. Especially being suspended from work for two weeks.

She chilled while Bones talked to the guy behind the counter about a gold chain that he was interested with.

It wasn't long before the guy walked in the back for somethinng and Bones made his way over to where she was standing at.

"I see you looking at this shit over here. What you like?"

Makyla pointed to a tennis bracelet. "I like this right here."

"That's it?" He asked, trying to see what type of girl she was.

"Yeah, that's it."

Bones walked away when the worker came back up front. They started discussing the price on the chain. Makyla couldn't really pay attention because her phone ringing had distracted her. She walked by Bones and told him that she would be right back. As she walked out, he finished taking care of his business.

"Hello."

"I know you mad at me about last night, but who the fuck is that nigga you with? I got muthafuckas calling me and shit about you!" Mehki yelled into the phone.

"Look, did you forget that I'm grown?" She asked with an attitude.

"Whatever, sis, I see you erased that shit, before I could see it. Don't get no nigga fucked up!" Mekhi yelled.

She didn't even waste her time arguing with him, she simply hung up the phone. He should have been lucky that she even answered for his ass.

Just as she was putting her phone away, Bones jumped in the car. "Did you tell your lil boyfriend you were spending the day with me?"

"Stop playing with me, Brandon. That was my brother's crazy ass."

"Yeah, yeah, tell me anything."

Makyla moved closer towards him, then placed a kiss on his lips. "I love you."

Bones once again didn't say anything. For a moment, he was stuck. She sat back in her seat. It bothered her not knowing what was on his mind.

"Damn, Makyla, you gon' have to stop that shit."

She gave him a confused look. "Stop what?"

"Telling me that shit. Look, I'm gonna be honest with you. I'm a street nigga, a straight up thug, and I don't really believe in all that love shit. I'm really not the type of nigga that you need to waste those feelings on."

"You sound crazy as hell, Brandon. You can't just turn your feelings off like that. Plus, you're a good guy."

"Nah, I ain't shit, and you shouldn't love me. Thanks doe."

Although he was serious, she just didn't want to listen to what he was saying. Her feelings were already developed for him. Trying to change the subject and not hurt her feelings, Bones pulled out a small square box from his bag.

"Give me your arm," he ordered.

She held out her left arm as he placed the bracelet that she was checking out on her.

"Thank you, baby," she said before giving him a kiss.

Since they had been seeing each other, he always surprised her with gifts. That was a reason that she knew deep down inside he did have feelings for her no matter what he was saying.

"That looks nice on you," he said before starting the car.

"Thank you. I really love it, baby."

Bones continued to drive. He knew it killed her not knowing where they were going, but he didn't want to scare her. He bent a couple of corners before pulling up in a driveway to a nice sized home.

"Come on, get your ass out." Makyla gave him a crazy look. "Whose house is this, Brandon?"

"Come see."

Makyla nervously got of the truck and followed him onto the porch. He rang the doorbell and waited for his mom to open the door. His mom wanted to meet Makyla so bad that he was about to make that happen.

April opened the door. "Boy, it's about time you made it here. The food almost done."

Makyla hit Bones. "Why you didn't tell me we were coming over your mom's house?"

He laughed as they walked into the house.

"Ma, this right here is Makyla. Makyla, this is my mama, April."

Makyla shyly said hi, but she was surprised when April pulled her in for a hug. "You don't have to be shy around me, girl."

Bones wanted to tell his mom that she was shy and the only time she wasn't was when there were fucking but decided not to embarrass her like that.

April took a step back and gave Makyla a good look. "Ok, girl. I can see why my son feeling you. You got his ass wide open."

Makyla laughed. She could tell that she was very outspoken and so was her son.

"Ma, stop all that shit. What you cookin', it smells good in here?" Bones asked, trying to change the subject.

"I got some corn beef, cabbage, cornbread, yams, and some mac & cheese cooking. It should be ready in a minute."

"That all sounds so good," Makyla said.

Everyone took a seat in the living room and talked while waiting to eat.

"So, Makyla, do you have any kids?"

"Damn, ma!" Bones yelled.

"What? I'm just trying to get to know my future daughter-in-law. I'm sorry if I offended you, I'm just not use to meeting his female friends. His ass used to be fucking all types of bitches in my house and sneaking them out. You the first one that I actually met. You must got my baby wrapped around your finger."

Makyla couldn't help but to laugh at his mom. She was silly, just like her son.

"Ma, if I knew you were gonna try to embarrass me, I would have kept her away from you."

"I'm sorry, Bones. You know sometimes I can't control my mouth," April admitted.

Soon, the food was ready and plates were made. Makyla wasted no time stuffing her face.

"This food is so good, Ms. April."

"Thanks, I'm just happy to cook for someone else other than my greedy ass son."

Both ladies looked over to Bones who was already damn near done with his plate. April couldn't help herself when she turned and asked Makyla if she was feeding her son.

Bones couldn't help but to laugh and before Makyla answered, he spoke up. "Yeah, ma, she be feeding a nigga all the time."

Makyla tried not to laugh, but he was just so stupid at times. "Baby, cut it out."

April gave her son a funny look. "I can't stand your nasty ass. That's exactly why I buy plastic forks and shit."

Makyla was really cracking up now. Them two together was a comedy show.

"So, Makyla, what do you do, honey?"

"Right now, I work at a clothing store in the mall, and I also attend a community college. I'm taking up business and once I'm done with my classes, I'm praying that I have enough saved to go into business for myself. I design clothes and want my own store."

"Ok, I like you. I see you got a good head on your shoulders. I like how you already got your future planned out."

Bone put his plate in the sink. "Yeah, ma, she smart ass hell. Sometimes I be up when she's doing her homework and shit."

Makyla blushed as he bragged about her.

"Anyways," April said before turning her attention back to her future daughter-in-law.

"So, you say you don't have any kids, but my question is, do you plan on giving my son any babies? I'm not getting any younger and would love a grand baby or two."

Her question almost made Makyla choke on her food. Bones shook his head at his mama, wishing that she would shut the hell up.

"Um, excuse me," Makyla said, making her way towards the bathroom.

"Ma I'm gonna need you to chill out. Me and Makyla cool and all, but we ain't together like that. And you know I'm not trying to have kids and shit. You gon' have her thinking its more to us than it is."

"I know you fucking lying, boy, talking about y'all not together like that. I know the only reason you let me meet her is because she is the one for you. Stop playing with me. I hope you not playing with that girl feelings," April said, raising her voice a little.

"Ma, calm down, she knows exactly what it is."

"Whatever. I see the way she looks at you. That girl been bitten by the love bug."

Before Bones could respond, Makyla walked back into the kitchen. As she grabbed her plate from off the table, she looked over at April. "That food was so good and thanks for inviting me over for a meal."

"Thanks, baby. You know you're welcome over here anytime. Even if it's without his stupid ass."

Bones could tell that his mom was pissed, and it was time to go. If they stayed, she was gonna keep throwing shots, and he was gonna be forced to throw some back.

"Makyla, you ready?" Bones asked.

"Sure."

They all said their goodbyes and gave out hugs. The ride home was quiet. Bones was busy thinking about that shit his mama was talking while Makyla was trying hard not to be all in her feelings.

Once inside of his crib, he tried to hug her, but she pushed him off her. "Leave me alone, Brandon."

He stepped back and watched her grab her shit that was in his room. She was packing her shit up and ready to go back home.

"What the fuck is your problem?"

"I don't have a fucking problem!" She yelled right back at him.

He tried to grab her arm and pull her down on his lap. "What's wrong, baby? Talk to me."

"Ain't no point of talking. I know what's the deal with us."

Bones tried to play dumb. "Fuck you talking about?"

"I heard you and your mama talking. So, we not together like that, huh?"

Bones shook his head. "Makyla, what the fuck you are tripping for? We doin' us, what the fuck we need titles for?"

"I'm not used to just being somebody's fuck toy!" She yelled.

"Well, you should have said something before you took that position. We never discussed being in a fucking relationship."

Makyla shook her head. She couldn't believe what he was saying. After gathering her stuff, she placed the bracelet on his dresser and quietly walked out. She wasn't about to tolerate his bullshit. She had already dealt with her ex's bullshit for so long. She tried to hold herself together, but once in the car, she broke down and cried.

She felt foolish for falling for him and believing that he wanted her.

Bones wasn't into chasing a bitch. Most of the time, he didn't even chase his liquor. He went into the kitchen grabbed his Henny out the freezer. He thought about grabbing a lil glass but decided to just kill the bottle. He made his way to the living room, climbed in his recliner then turned on the game.

"Stupid ass bitch," he mumbled.

CHAPTER 5

MAKAYLA

Although Makyla didn't want to stay at that house anymore, she had no other choice. For the last two weeks that she had been off of work, she had been looking for a new job. She knew that moving was gonna take up all of her money, so she pushed her dreams of buying her own building to the side. She felt sad knowing that she had to do that because of her surroundings.

That whole two weeks that she was off, she didn't talk to Bones. She pulled out her phone a few times to call him but quickly put the phone down. She wasn't nobody's jump off and wasn't gonna allow a nigga to treat her like one. Not only had she been ignoring Bones, she also barely said anything to her brothers. She tried her best to stay away from the house.

As she looked into her mirror, she told herself that she deserved better and was smart and beautiful enough to find someone else.

As she walked out into the living room, Mike was sitting on the couch chilling. It surprised her that he was even out of the room. She wanted to ask him how he was doing. Since that night, he hadn't been the same. She stared at him for a minute, then walked out of the door. If he couldn't speak then she wasn't either.

***

"Welcome back, Makyla," Hanna said as she walked into the store.

"Hey," she said dryly. She wasn't fucking with them muthafuckas at that job anymore. They were all on her shit list.

For the first half of her shift, she took care of her customers and didn't say much to no one. On her break, she got her a slice of pizza and a bottle of water. She took a seat at a table in the back, trying to enjoy her break.

"What's up, Makyla? How's everything going?" Dontae asked.

Dontae worked at the shoe store in the mall. They talked from time to time and she had asked him earlier if he could pull her in to his job.

"Hey, Dontae. I'm good, just been trying to keep to myself so I won't have to go off on them muthafuckas in that bitch."

"Damn, girl, you so fucking mean," he said, laughing.

Makyla finally laughed. She had been walking around with the resting bitch face all day. Dontae looked up from his food and just as he was about to say something, he noticed someone walking over towards their table. Bones leaned over Makyla, placing a kiss on her cheek. He then took a seat next to her, never taking his eyes of the nigga sitting in her face.

"What's up, girl?" Bones asked, finally looking at her.

"What are you doing here?" She asked.

Bone hated how she didn't answer his question and decided to act an ass. He gave her another kiss, this time on her lips. "Fuck is this nigga?"

"Brandon, this is Dontae. He works here in the mall."

Bones laughed, "Do it look like I really give a fuck? I was just wondering why the fuck he still sitting here."

Dontae didn't want any problems with the crazy guy sitting across from him, so he decided to just leave. Dontae grabbed his food. "I think it would be best if you talk to my boss on your own."

Makyla rolled her eyes, "Ok."

Once Dontae was out of sight, Makyla turned in her seat to face Bones. "What the fuck is your problem? Why the fuck are you coming up here on that bullshit?"

"I missed your mean ass. Why the fuck haven't I heard from you in two weeks?" Bones asked, rubbing on her thighs.

Makyla moved his hands off her. "Don't touch me, Brandon. I'm not your woman, remember?"

"I was sucking and licking on that fat ass pussy when you wasn't my woman, and you wasn't complaining then. Why you gotta be trippin' now?"

She shook her head. He was so fucking ignorant, and it made no sense at all. "Look, it's time for me to get back to work, so bye."

Makyla tried to get up to leave, but he held on to her arm. "My mama asked about you. I told her you weren't fucking with me no more."

He then grabbed her phone and put his mom's number in her phone. "Give her a call so she can go off on you for breaking my heart."

"Whatever, Brandon, you so full of shit," she said, now laughing at his crazy ass.

"Go tell your boss you gotta leave and roll out with me," he ordered.

Makayla hated how she was able to ignore him for two weeks just to feel all mushy inside seeing him face to face. It was crazy how she told herself that she didn't need him, yet she was sitting there entertaining the thought of leaving with him. She sat there arguing with herself on what to do.

"I can't leave. You do remember that I was suspended for two weeks, and I need all the money I can get for my new place."

"You still having problems with your people?" He asked.

"Yes, and that's why I was talking to that guy. I was trying to get him to pull me in to his job. I have too much that I wanna do to be worried about holding on to that job at that clothing store."

"Come stay with me," Bones suddenly blurted out.

"Whatever, stop playing with me, boy."

"I'm serious, baby. Come stay with me. All you gotta do is fuck me and feed me."

Makyla laughed, not taking him seriously. Bones grabbed her face so she could look into his eyes. "I'm not playing. If you don't wanna be where you at, my door is always open for you."

"Ok, Brandon. I'll think about it. Now I really have to go before they start calling my phone looking for me."

Bones stood up from his seat jut as she did. He gave her a hug making sure to give her ass a squeeze. "Damn, I missed squeezing on that fat muthafucka."

She hit him in the arm while laughing. "Boy, shut up."

"For real, when you get off, come to my place."

"Ok, dang."

He then gave her a key. "I got to go handle some business, so if I'm not home, just let yourself in."

Makyla gave him one last kiss before walking off to her job. Honestly, she did miss his crazy ass and couldn't wait to see him later on.

For the remaining four hours, Makyla found herself watching the clock. Soon as it was time for her to go, she hurried to clock out.

"Makyla, before you leave, I was wondering if you could stay for the last three hours?" Mr. Dickerson asked.

"Nope, I have to go," she quickly said.

"Well, you been gone for two weeks. Don't you need to make that money up?" He asked, getting on her nerves.

"Nah, I'm good, but enjoy the rest of your day."

***

Makyla pulled out her phone, dialing Bones' number to see where he was at.

"Hey, baby, where are you? I just got off," she said into the phone after the fourth ring.

Bones looked around at the situation he was in.

"Hey, baby, just go straight to the crib and give me aboutan hour," he said, making his boys look at him as if he wascrazy.

Once he hung up the phone and slipped it in his pocket, he walked back over to stand on the plastic that was placed on the floor. There was a guy tied down to a chair half ass dead, begging him to let him live.

"My bad, you know when the wife calls, I gotta answer."

Gunna and Choppa laughed at their boy.

"Damn, dog, you crazy as hell," Gunna said as he handed him his bat.

"Go ahead and finish this bitch off," Choppa ordered.

That's all Bones needed to hear before knocking the guy in the head with the bat. "Bitch ass nigga. I bet you won't try to run off with nobody else money."

Although the guy was dead now, Bones hit him twice more. "Ok, y'all, I gotta get cleaned up before I go home. Call them niggas and have them clean up this mess."

They both looked at him strangely before Gunna finally asked, "So you got a wifey now, nigga?"

Bones chuckled, "Man, get out my business. As long as I'm not fucking your bitch, you have nothing to worry about."

Bones walked out of the abandoned warehouse and made his way to him mom's house. He couldn't go home and let Makyla see him with blood all over him. Knowing her son and his life style, she didn't say shit as he walked in the house and jumped started the shower. While he was in the bathroom, she opened the door, then placed a black trash bag on the sink for his bloody clothes. This was a routine that she was familiar with.

Once out of the bathroom, Bones went into his room that he had there and got dressed.

"Ma, I'm about to head home," he said, walking in the living room.

"Ok, Bones, but I want you to be careful out here in the street. You know that bitch Karma don't play fair with nobody."

"Yeah, ma, I'm always careful," he said, hating when she borught up Karma and shit.

"Did you tell Makyla to call me?"

Bones chuckled, "Yeah, I did tell her to call so you can go off on her mean ass for breaking my heart. That's probably why she ain't call yet."

Although she laughed at her son, she couldn't help but to shake her head. "Boy, if anything, I need to go off on you for playing with that girl's feelings. I told you that I could tell by the way she looked at you that she loved your crazy ass."

"I know she loves me, she be telling me that shit," he admitted.

"Ok, and did you say it back? 'Cause it's obvious that you feel the same way."

"Ma, you are tripping. I'm gonna tell you the same thing I told her ass. I'm a fucking thug, we don't do that love shit."

April gave her son a mean look. "Ok, get your stupid ass from out my damn house. Fuck all that thug and street shit. You gon' run that girl away."

"Bye, ma. I'll call you in the morning. Your ass tripping right now."

Bones gave his mom a hug, although she fought him off her before leaving. She loved her son, but she didn't like his way of thinking.

***

Makyla walked into Bones' apartment and was surprised to see a bouquet of flowers and some balloons. Some were heart shaped and some just said *I missed you,* but none said *I love you. At least he tried,* she thought to herself. She then went into the kitchen and made it her business to cook them something to eat. She wanted him to come home to a nice, home cooked meal, so they could relax afterwards.

About time dinner was done, Bones was walking into the door. He smiled knowing that his baby was back into his life. He tried to act cool without her, but truthfully, those were the longest two weeks ever. He wasn't sure what was worse, doing those five years or being without her little sexy ass.

"Honey, I'm home!" He yelled as he made his way to the kitchen.

She had her music playing and didn't hear him. He stood in the doorway watching her twerk her ass while pulling some potatoes out of the oven.

Once she turned around, she jumped. "Damn, baby, you scared me. I didn't hear you come in."

"I see. Your ass was too busy shaking that ass all over the fucking kitchen."

"Whatever, go wash your hands so you can come eat," she ordered.

Bones didn't like taking orders, but since they were coming from her, he did what she said do. He quickly returned to the dining room to take a seat at the table.

As she sat their plates down on the table, Bones stared at his plate. "Man, this shit looks good. I hope you ain't trying to poison a nigga. I know the last time you were here, I pissed you off."

"Stop bringing up old stuff unless you're ready to apologize."

"Let me shut up then."

Makyla couldn't help but to laugh at his rude ass.

"I missed your crazy ass, I swear."

"I missed your beautiful ass too. Since you here, does that mean you moving in?"

"I told you I was gonna think about it. I never lived with a guy before and don't wanna just jump into something, especially when it's not my man or someone who really doesn't want a future with me," she coldly said, knowing it would bother him.

Bones got up from the table to put his plate in the sink. Without saying anything else to her, he walked away. He was pissed, but she didn't do shit but bring up the shit he had told her before.

Makyla sat at the table and finished eating her dinner. Hearing her phone beep, letting her know that she had a new text, she got up to grab it off the counter.

Justice: Bitch, what you doing? Wanna hit up a bar tonight?

Makyla smiled at the text. Justice was always trying to get her to go out. She quickly texted Justice back.

Makyla: Idk yet, chilling with my dude right now. If he be on some bullshit, I'll hit you up later.

Shortly, Justice texted right back.

Justice: Ok, bitch, just let me know. And when can I meet your dude? You've been holding out on me.

After cleaning the kitchen, Makyla made her way into the bathroom to take a shower. She was giving Bones all the time that he needed to get out his feelings. It felt good to feel the warm water hit her body. After her long day at work, she was ready to go to bed. Justice was gonna be mad at her, but she was gonna make it up to her soon.

Bones opened the bathroom door just as Makyla was wrapping her towel around her body. "Don't be walking in on me, boy."

He didn't even respond. Bones rude ass just pulled his dick out and took a piss. Makyla shook her head while walking out. She forgot that she took all her clothes home and now she didn't have anything to stick on. She opened up his drawer to find a t- shirt.

"Why you in my shit?" Bones asked from the doorway.

Makyla turned around. "Baby, I don't have nothing to sleep in, so I was looking for a shirt.

"You sound crazy as hell. You not getting in my bed with no fucking clothes on. You ready to lay down now?"

Dropping her towel told him everything that he needed to know. He smiled looking over her perfect body. She had to be crazy to think that he wasn't gonna wanna touch on her.

"So, my bestie wants me to go out with her tonight. I was thinking about taking a nap, then going home to pick up an outfit."

Bones watched as she climbed in the bed next to him. "Who said you could go out?"

"Boy, bye. I'm not about to play no games with you. I don't have to ask permission, you not my man or my daddy."

"Shid, I had your ass screaming daddy plenty of times. So, what the fuck you talkin' 'bout?"

"I swear you are so crazy."

It was a moment of silence before she finally decided to get serious with him. "Why did you want me to come over here if you were gonna be acting like an ass all night? Do you even really want me to be here or were you just trying to see if I would come running back to you and say fuck standing my ground of being done with you?"

Bones laid his head back on the headboard. He looked frustrated and confused. It had taken him a second before he opened his mouth to say anything.

"Look man, I wanted you here with me because I missed the fuck out of you. I never really just chilled with a female after I fucked unless I wanted more. Just being without you for those two weeks made me realize that I wanted you. So, that's why you here," Bones admitted.

"So basically, I'm here because you want some more pussy?" Makyla asked. She knew what he was really trying to say, or at least what she thought he meant but wanted him to just say it.

"Man, why the fuck you playing so much? You know what the fuck I'm talking about. I missed your mean ass."

Makyla swaddled Bones' lap. "I missed you too, baby. You really need to stop acting like thugs and street niggas can't have a heart. I know you got feelings for me and you're just scared to admit it."

"Man, Makyla, I ain't scared of shit, muthafucka," Bones said with a smile on his face.

Makyla thought it was funny that he was acting like a lil boy with a crush. "Ok, I'm about to go home then," she said as she tried to get off his lap.

He held on to her tighter. "Stop playing with me, for real. You know you my baby so stop acting crazy and shit."

Bones managed to lift her up long enough to pull his dick out of his boxers. She slowly allowed his dick to rip her open as she went down.

"Damn, ain't no way you done grew."

"Shut your goofy ass up and take that dick."

Makyla did exactly what he ordered her to do. In only a few minutes, they were all over the bed fucking like wild animals. They both missed each other, and it showed.

"Damn, baby, I love you," she moaned out with no problem.

Justice, Makyla, & Bones

"Bitch, where the fuck you find that nigga at? He is fine as hell," Justice said to Makyla once Bones went to go get them some drinks.

Makyla was all smiles and couldn't help but to blush. "Girl, he walked into my job one day, and we been together since. I really, I mean really, really like him," she admitted.

Makayla had talked Bones into going out with her and Justice. He agreed to go, but only if they went to his people's spot.

"Aww boo, look at your face glowing and shit. He just might be the one. So, have your brothers met him yet?"

"Hell nah, so please don't say shit, especially to Mehki."

"Girl, I'm not fucking with him no more. He thinks he's just gonna pop up and fuck me, but don't want to commit to me. So, since I'm single, I'm doing single shit. Plus, my mama got Lil Man for a few days."

"Ayyyyee! Bitch turn up!" Makyla yelled right before Bones walked over to their table.

"Man, don't start all that aye and that other loud shit y'all be yelling," he said, taking a seat.

"Shut up, baby, we just trying to have a good time."

Justice didn't say anything, but from that moment, she didn't like him anymore. She could tell that he was rude and very demanding. She was gonna vouch for him just because he was fine, but she didn't want her best friend with that nigga. She was sort of a good girl and didn't need a nigga like him bringing her down.

"My auntie gon' be over to take orders if anyone's hungry."

Justice turned her attention to Bones. "So, this your people's spot?" She asked.

"Yeah, her and my uncle's," he answered.

Makyla sipped on her drink, in her own little world. It was only her fourth time there, but she loved it there. That spot had become her favorite hangout spot.

"Damn, Makyla, when did you start drinking?"

"Damn, Mama Justice, I'm grown. You know?" Makyla answered with a slight attitude.

Bones looked up to see his auntie making her way towards their table.

"Hey, Makyla. I swear every time I see you in here, you're even prettier and you just a glowing. That could only mean my nephew been doing you right."

Makyla blushed. "Thank you and yes, he's been everything to me."

Noticing that Justices was across the room rolling her eyes, Makyla made it her business to introduce her. "Hey, Auntie Cookie, this is my best friend, Justice. And Justice, this is Bones' Auntie Cookie."

The two shook hands and gave off a fake smile.

"So, have y'all decided what y'all wanna eat?" Auntie Cookie asked.

"You already know we want some wings. Baby you want your fries and salad?" Bones asked, placing his and his date's order.

"Not really, baby, I'm really not feeling that tonight. With the wings can I get some spaghetti, corn on the cob, and-"

"Damn, we did eat a few hours ago, greedy ass-" Bones said, cutting her off.

"Boy, leave me alone. I'm hungry again. Spaghetti and the corn would do. What do you want, Justice?"

"I'll have some hot wings and fries," she quickly said.

Aunt Cookie wrote down everyone's order before walking away.

"Come on, Justice, let's go dance while we wait on our food."

Before Justice could even say no, Makyla was pulling her up by the arm. As they danced, Bones watched his girl move on the floor. He was enjoying himself but would have been fine without her friend. It was something about her that rubbed him the wrong way. He was gonna let them enjoy their night, but he was honestly debating on if he should speak his mind. He usually did, but with this situation and that being her best friend, he didn't want to piss her off.

"So, what's the problem?" Makyla finally asked her bestie.

"Girl, what the fuck you doing with that nigga? You talk all that shit about your brothers being thugs and street niggas, but you went out and found you one. What the fuck is up with that?"

Makyla stepped back from her friend. "You right, he is a thug, but I love him. If you're gonna start acting funny and keep giving us the death stare, maybe you should just leave."

Justice snapped, "Look at you, bitch, all in your fucking feelings and shit. That nigga got you dick dumb, clearly."

"Whatever. You in my fucking face like you and my brother got the perfect relationship, and we both know that ain't true."

Not wanting to ruin her night, Makyla took it upon herself to just walk away. When she returned to the table, Bones gave her a funny look, wondering if she was gonna tell him what went down.

Seeing that she was quiet and looking upset, he said fuck waiting, "Aye baby, what's up with you and your girl?"

"Nothing."

"Well don't sit in my face looking like that. You know this our chill spot."

Makyla gave him a fake smile. "You right, baby. I'm not about to let nothing ruin our night."

Justice walked out of the restroom feeling a little better. She said what she had to say and that was it. If Makyla was mad, then oh fucking well.

"Damn, Justice, your nigga let you out of his eye sight?" Lamar asked.

Lamar was a guy from her neighborhood that had been trying to hook up with her for the longest. He knew Mehki wasn't the right nigga to fuck with, but if she had let him fuck and didn't tell, he wouldn't either.

"Stop playing with me. I'm single as hell. I have a baby daddy, not a fucking man," she said with so much pride.

"You single, huh? Well in that case, why don't we get the fuck from out here and have some fun? You know I've been waiting for that pussy for the longest."

Justice looked over at the table and saw her friend and her so called boyfriend laughing, eating and enjoying their selves. "Let me go get my bag, and we can leave."

Lamar watched as she went over towards the table. He couldn't wait to fuck that bitch, especially since her nigga thought he had her on lock, and she was so fucking untouchable.

"So, I'm about to leave. I'm really not feeling this place. I'll call you later, Makyla." Just like that, Justice walked off.

"Damn, that bitch tripping. What's that all about?"

Makyla stopped eating her food. "Baby, I don't wanna lie to you, but she doesn't like you and feels like I shouldn't waste my time on somebody like you."

"Damn really? Well, you know how I feel, fuck that bitch." Bones laughed before asking, "So, how do you feel?"

Makyla playfully hit his arm. "Stop acting crazy. You know how I feel, baby. I tell you all the time that I love your ass."

"Yeah, your hard-headed ass do, even when I tell you to stop that shit. I keep telling you niggas like me ain't shit and you shouldn't waste your love on me."

"Oh my gawd, boy, I wish you stop talking so fucking stupid like that. I really hate that shit. You know what, I take it back, I don't love you. Now can we finish our date?"

Bones didn't say shit.

Mehki & Justice

Mehki used his keys to open Justice's front door. For three days straight, he had been calling her, and she had been avoiding him. As he opened the door and walked in, he tried to calm down because he was pissed to the point that he wanted to kill her. After walking around and checking his son's room, he was glad to see that he was still with his grandma. He then opened up Justice's bedroom door where he found her in the dark with her head buried under the cover.

"Justice, get your ass up!" He yelled, pulling the cover off her.

"What, Mehki? What the fuck do you want?" She yelled back.

"So, why the fuck you ain't been answering the fucking phone? And I heard you were talking to some nigga in the club the other night."

"Mehki, you're not my man and I don't have to answer for you. Plus, I can talk to whoever. And instead of being in my fucking business, you need to be worried about that thug nigga your sister fucking with!" She yelled, pissing him off.

"Oh, so you back on that bullshit? So, tell me, is this your man?" Mehki pulled out his phone and played the video that was sent to him. Her shit was deeper than worrying about Makyla right now.

Justice instantly burst into tears seeing herself get roughly fucked by Lamar. "Oh my gawd, Mehki! I'm so sorry, baby. I didn't know he was taping us."

"Fuck you sorry for, bitch? You knew you were giving that pussy away. You see, this is the exact reason why I wasn't in a rush to commit."

Justice continued to cry her eyes out while begging for forgiveness. "I'm so sorry, baby. Please, Mehki, you have to forgive me."

After the last time they had got into it, Mehki had planned on making shit official and even brought her a ring to prove that he was serious. Some shit ended up popping up in the streets, and he got caught up. About time he cleared shit up and was ready to come see her, her sex tape was sent to his phone. He loved her but at this point, he wasn't sure if he would ever be able to look at her the same.

"Forgive you? Bitch, watch this fucking tape. How could I forgive you for this shit?"

Justice watched as Lamar tied her hands up to the headboard and blindfolded her. He was driving her wild. She was moaning and screaming out, calling him daddy and shit. Then he pulled out and stepped back. Justice laid on the bed begging for more dick. Just then, a second guy was seen taking Lamar's place. The two-nigga slapped five before the second guy stuffed his dick in her mouth.

"Oh no! No! No! No! That is not what I wanted! Oh, my gawd!" She cried out.

Mehki stood up from the bed, snatching his phone from her. "Have my son call me when he come home."

"Mehki, please. Please, baby, don't leave me. I'm so sorry, baby."

Before walking out of the door, Mehki turned around to face her. "You know what, Justice, I really did love your ass. I even paid your mom to keep Li' Man a few more days so I could ask you to marry me. I wanted us to celebrate while he was gone so it could just be the two of us, but you had to be on that *I'm single shit* and go out and get you some dick. I hope you like what you got.

"No, Mehki! Please, I'll do anything to fix us. Please don't leave me." She continued to cry.

"All you had to do was sit your ass down and wait on a nigga. That's all the fuck I asked you to do, Justice."

As he turned around to walk out, Justice could have sworn that she saw tears in his eyes. She knew then that he would never forgive her. Hearing the front door slam made her cry even harder. Her life was now over. Justice thought about how she had been filmed fucking and sucking two nigga's dicks and it made her sick to her stomach. She hurried to the bathroom where she vomited in the toilet.

CHAPTER 6

MIKE

Mike knocked on Roni's door, hoping she wasn't on no bullshit because he hadn't been calling her. Opening up the door, she rolled her eyes but allowed him to come in.

"Glad to know you're ok," she said, flopping down on the couch.

Mike took a seat next to her. "Why wouldn't I be? I told you I was gonna handle that nigga, didn't I?"

Roni put her head down. She was happy that Rell was gone and out her life. Him being a hoe ass nigga and raping her a few months ago had her scared and living in a bubble, although Mike had told her not to worry about it. Getting comfortable on the couch, Mike was stuck in his thoughts. The day he found out Rell had raped his girl was as clear as day.

Roni had been his girl for a good eight months now, and he could say that he had strong feelings for her. He would even go all the way to say that he loved her ass. He had been out in the streets the day before and wanted to come check on her. Once she opened the door, he instantly could tell that she had been crying. At first, he thought that she was mad because he hadn't been answering her calls, but really, he had lost his phone two days ago hooping at the gym.

"My bad, baby, I know I was supposed to call, but I lost my phone and was caught up yesterday. You see, I got up this morning and came straight over here to see you."

Roni took a seat on the couch but was still upset. Mike took a seat next to her. As he reached over to give her a hug, he could feel her shaking like she was scared or something.

"What's up with you, Roni?"

Not able to talk, she looked up at him then started to cry.

Mike jumped up from the couch. "Man, what the fuck going on, girl?"

Roni then stood up herself. She was still crying but hugged onto Mike so he would calm down. She hated when he blew up.

"Baby, have a seat so I can talk to you."

They both then took a seat back on the couch. "What's up, man? All that crying got me worried."

Roni took a deep breath. "Mike, I'm so scared to tell you this, but the longer I hold it in, the more I hurt."

Sitting back now, he had a worried look on his face. "Go ahead, baby. Let me know what's going on."

"I went to the doctor yesterday, and he told me that I was eleven weeks pregnant," she managed to say without crying too hard.

Mike gave her a hug. "Fuck you crying for? That's good news, right? You don't wanna have my baby?"

"I would love to have your baby, Mike, but I have to tell you something else. Do you remember when me and my cousins went out for Shay's birthday?"

"Yeah, I remember, but what the fuck that got to do with you being pregnant?"

Roni put her head on his chest and cried. "Baby, I danced with this guy that I went to school with, and I was so stupid, baby."

Mike pushed her off him, thinking that she was about to tell him that she fucked another nigga and was now pregnant. "Man, what the fuck you sayin', Roni?"

She could tell by his tone that from jump, he was thinking that she was a cheating hoe.

"Wait, baby, I swear it wasn't shit like that. I would never play you like that. I love you, Mike."

Mike wanted to say it back, but first he wanted to know what the fuck was really going on.

"He asked me if I wanted to go outside and smoke. Being so stupid, I said yeah. I didn't think much of it because like I said, we had known each other for some years now. Well, we were outside smoking and just talking about bullshit that happened in school."

Roni took a quick pause as she tried to calm herself down. "Baby, he attacked me. I swear I tried to fight him off me, but I couldn't. He raped me, baby," she cried out.

Most girls would lie, but by the way she cried and the way her body shook, he knew that she was telling the truth. He was just as pissed as her and knew that soon as she calmed down, he was gonna get the name of the muthafucka he was gonna have to get rid of.

Not wanting her to feel even more fucked up, Mike took his seat back then pulled her into his arms. "It's ok, Roni. I'm here for you no matter what."

Hearing him say that touched her heart, but that was why she loved him. Mike was a good guy and always had her back.

The young couple ended up cuddled on the couch for the rest of the afternoon watching Netflix. She had dozed off from all the crying, but he was wide awake thinking about what she had told him.

He reminisced back to around the time of her cousin's party. The days that followed that as he could remember, she was depressed and distant. For a while, she wouldn't even give him no pussy. He felt like shit not noticing that she was going thru something so serious. He hugged on her just a little tight before placing a kiss on her.

"I love you," he mumbled. A single tear rolled down Mike's eye. He knew that he was gonna have to catch his first body.

After finding out who it was, it had taken him three days to finally see the nigga face to face. When he did, he wasted no words on him. He beat the shit out of the nigga. The only reason he didn't kill him was because he had left his gun at the crib.

Rell pretended not to know who he was or what was going on, but he was no longer a problem for nobody.

"You hungry, Mike?" Roni asked, changing the subject.

"Yeah, what you cook?"

"I made some fried chicken wings and some spaghetti. Let me get up and fix your plate."

Mike sat up and watched her walk off to the kitchen. After having everything out in the clear, it was like their relationship got stronger and he could trust her with anything. She quickly came back with his plate and the bottle of hotsauce.

"Here you go, baby," she said, placing the plate down on the coffee table.

Before she could walk away, Mike pulled her towards him.

"What now, baby?"

Mike lifted her shirt up far enough to see her little pudge. He then gave her belly a kiss.

"I love y'all, man."

Roni giggled, "We love you too, daddy."

The young couple spent the rest of the afternoon together until Mehki called.

After kicking it with Mehki on the phone for a few minutes, he learned that he needed to go home. Some shit had popped up and Mehki was gonna come soop him up a little later.

"I really wish you didn't have to go, Mike, but I know business is business."

"Look, I'm just gonna have him pick me up from here and leave my car here. Once we done, I'll be right back. I promise, you got me all day tomorrow."

Roni was all smiles. She loved laying up with Mike. Plus, she loved the fact that he was still on her side no matter what.

Mehki

Mehki finally pulled up in front of Mike's girlfriend's house. He had only saw her a few times, but he was cool with that. She seemed to be a good girl for him. She seemed to keep him leveled. As you could see, after catching his first body, he was stuck in his room crying and shit. But as soon as he got his shit together, he ran straight to her ass. Mehki knew his lil bro was in love.

Pulling out his phone, Mehki called Mike.

"Aye, bro, climb out that pussy and come on out here," Mehki jokingly said into the phone.

Mike laughed, then hung up the phone. He turned his attention towards his girl, who was laying next to him. Placing a kiss on her, Mike climbed out the bed to put his clothes back on. Not feeling Mike any longer, Roni lifted up.

"Baby, you're about to go?" She asked, still half sleep.

"Yeah, bro just pulled up."

She sat up to receive one last kiss before he walked out the door.

Soon as Mike climbed in the car, Mehki started talking shit. "Damn nigga, it took you long enough to get out here. What the fuck, bro, don't tell me you were still in there fucking."

"Nah, bro, I dozed off after I got off the phone with you."

"On the real, bro, I'm just glad you're feeling better now. That whole Rell thing had you fucked up. I remember being like that when I had my first kill."

Mike really ain't wanna talk about it, but he was sort of happy that Mehki understood what had been going on with him.

Mehki continued to talk seeing Mike wasn't gonna say what he really wanted to know.

"You know niggas be having their reasons as to why another nigga gotta die. It really ain't my business, but what did Rell do?"

"You right, nigga, it really ain't your business. So, let's just keep it like that."

Mehki couldn't believe Mike was giving him an attitude when he was the one who helped kill Rell's homeboys.

"Nigga, I was with you that night and had your back like I should have, so you can tell me. I'm not trying to judge you. I'm just being nosey and trying to take my mind of the bullshit that went down."

Mike shook his head. He hated even thinking about what that nigga Rell did, but he knew his brother wasn't gonna drop the subject. "He did some hoe as shit to, Roni."

"Fuck you mean?"

Mike looked over towards Mehki, giving him a strange look.

"Oh, fuck nah, nigga! Are you fucking serious? Yeah, that nigga deserved to fucking die. Fuck that nigga!" Mehki yelled once he figured out what Mike was talking about.

Mike kept the whole baby shit out. He wasn't even trying to think about Rell being the daddy to the baby that him and Roni really wanted. It had taken them a minute to even decide for her not to get an abortion. The rest of the ride was somewhat quiet besides Yella Beezy blasting thru the speakers. Mehki's mind was on who he was gonna have to kill and how he was gonna make the money up that was stolen.

As they pulled up to their secret stash house, the brothers jumped out of the car.

"I had to call an important meeting. It's some new niggas around that's underestimating me and my killing skills," Mehki said as they walked in the house.

Once inside, Mehki looked around and saw that mostly everyone was there and waiting on them two.

"Ok, I'm gonna keep this shit short. From my understanding, some hoe ass niggas ran up in one of our spots and was able to run off with money, work and shot two workers."

Everyone looked around, but nobody said shit.

Mehki then turned around to address Big Ron. "Where the fuck was your fat ass at when shit popped off? You were supposed to be the one watching the house over there."

Big Ron shook his head. he was scared to tell the truth. Mehki wasn't for the bullshit. He pulled out his gun and pointed it at Big Ron, causing everyone that was around him to back up.

"Where the fuck was your fat ass?" He yelled again.

"I'm sorry, boss. I had gone around the corner to Coney Island. I got hungry."

Although two of their men were dead behind his fat ass being hungry, most of the workers laughed when he said he left because he was hungry.

"Hungry? Hungry? You fat slob!" Mehki yelled before pulling the trigger. That one bullet to his forehead dropped his ass.

"Y'all niggas clean this fat bitch up. Tomorrow, I want y'all to lay low while I do some investigation. I'm gonna kill whoever did this shit."

A few of the workers worked together to roll his fat ass up in a sheet to get him out of the house. The others left wondering who the fuck was brave enough to step to their crew.

Just as promised, Mike returned to Roni's house.

Mehki pulled up in front of Justice's house and just watched. Although she did agree to fucking that lame as nigga Lamar, he still felt bad for her. She didn't deserve to be played like that and he knew that the nigga only did that because they really ain't fuck with each other like that. He was what you would really call a fuck boy. He had already made up his mind that whenever he saw Lamar and his little boyfriend, he was gonna kill them both. He wasn't ready to talk to her, but at the same time, he missed her ass. His pride was in the way of him making shit right with her. After a minute or so, he started his car back up and drove off.

Mehki went home to an empty house. Mike was with his girl and since Justice had dry snitched on Makyla, he now knew she had a lil boyfriend. He couldn't wait to check her ass, but first, he needed to worry about his situation and how he was gonna handle his baby mama.

Just as he climbed in the bed, his phone started to ring. As he looked at the screen, he saw that it was Justice. Lately, he had been ignoring her, but being lonely and bored made him answer.

"Yeah. What's up?"

Justice wasn't sure what to say. She was surprised that he had even answered. "Hey, Mehki."

"What's up?" He asked again.

"I'm sorry about everything and I miss you, baby," she cried out.

Mehki shook his head. He missed her too, but the image of her being fucked by two niggas fucked with his mind.

"Look Justice, I'm really not trying to hold the phone and listen to you cry."

"Well the next time you pull up in front of my house, why don't you just come in and see if I'm ok," she snapped back.

Mehki had no idea that she knew that he had been stopping by every night. "Is my son there?" He asked, changing the subject.

"No, my mom still has him. She said she'll bring him home tomorrow afternoon," she answered.

"Have him call me when he gets there."

Before he could hang up, Justice called out for him. "Mehki."

"What?"

"I really am sorry, and I pray that one day soon we can look past this. I love you more than I love myself and can't see myself living without you."

Honestly, Mehki felt the same way about her, but instead of being a man and telling her the truth, he simply told her that he would call her back. As he laid back in the bed, he thought that maybe he would feel better once them niggas were dead and gone.

CHAPTER 7
MAKAYLA

"Damn, baby. What time you gon' get your ass up and get ready for school?" Bones asked while trying to wake Makyla up.

"I'm not going today."

"Why not? You not about to start fucking up in school 'cause you been staying over here with me."

"Baby, leave me alone, I don't feel good," she whined.

"So, you not going to work either?" He asked, taking a seat on the end of the bed.

"No. I really don't feel good. I'll call off in a minute."

Bones cuddled up with her. She never called off and always went to school, so he believed that something was really wrong with her.

Makyla sat up in the bed. "Oh my gawd!" She yelled before taking off running to the bathroom. She made it just in time to the toilet.

Bones sat up in the bed but didn't go follow her. Just the sound of her vomiting made his stomach feel sour.

"Man, what the fuck," he mumbled as he wondered what the fuck was wrong with her sick ass.

After brushing her teeth and washing her face, Makyla returned to the room. She then climbed back in the bed with Bones. He gave her a strange look.

"Man, get your nasty ass out my bed."

"Leave me alone, Bones. I don't feel like playing with your ass."

He laughed. "Fuck wrong with your ass?"

"I don't know. I think it's from that food we ate last night."

"I hope not. I can't be in this bitch sick like your ass. As a matter of fact, I'm about to go take my ass on the couch."

Makyla watched as he snatched up one of the pillows. "I swear you so fucking childish."

After he left, she picked her phone back up to call off.

"Hey, Hanna. Where's Mr. Dickerson?"

Hanna put her on hold for a second. Makyla just hoped that he wasn't on no bullshit because she wasn't in the mood for his shit today.

Mr. Dickerson got on the phone. "What can I do for you, Makyla?"

"I was calling to tell you that I'm really sick, and I need to call off today."

"Oh really? I'm sorry. but I don't have anyone to cover your shift, so you have to come in."

Makyla rolled her eyes at the phone, wishing he could see her. "Look, I never called off before and I always stay to help out. I really can't come in today."

"Ok, fine. You're fired!" He blurted out.

She was pissed and started to yell. "That's some bullshit and you know it. I called more than three hours ahead of time. Plus, I never done anything wrong!"

"I have the final word and you're fired. Pick up your last check Friday!" He yelled before hanging up.

Bones heard her yelling and was quick on his feet. As he stood on the side of the bed, he could see that she was on the edge of crying. "Fuck wrong with you?"

"Everything is just so fucked up for me," she cried.

"Who done pissed you off? What the fuck happened?"

"I just tried to call off and the stupid muthafucka fired me."

"Man, fuck that faggot ass nigga. You want me to go handle him?"

Makyla shook her head *yeah*. "I hate him, and he knew what I was working for."

Little did she know it, but just that quick, she signed his death certificate. "Don't cry, baby. I'm gonna handle everything."

"He allows everyone else to call off but fires me when I do it. I need another job, or I'll never get my store."

Bones placed a kiss on her lips. "Don't worry about it. We're gonna figure some shit out. Now wipe them punk ass tears away."

Makyla giggled as she wiped her tears away. "You just kissed me, now you got my cooties."

"Man, now you gotta suck that shit out of me," He said, pulling his dick out and placing the tip on her lips.

"I can't stand your ass, Brandon."

"Whatever. Go ahead and get to work before I get sick."

Although he was full of shit, Makyla did exactly what he wanted her to do. That was her man and she was happy with him being just the way that he was.

Bones' phone started to ring right as Makyla was finish and on her way to the bathroom. She loved Bones, but she wasn't a big fan of swallowing. He didn't give a fuck as long as she got that shit from out of him. He looked at the screen and saw that it was Choppa. So, he knew it was about business.

"What's up, nigga?"

"Aye, my nigga, we hit a nice ass lick yesterday. I can't wait to take care of their other places."

"Hell yeah, nigga. Them hoe ass nigga were caught sleeping. But anyways, did you split that work up to our boys?"

"Just got done doing that shit. We good my baby."

"Cool. I'll holla at you later."

Makyla climbed back in the bed.

"Aye, you hungry?"

"It's crazy because I am a little, but I don't wanna eat and get sick again," she answered

"I'm about to go to Coney. I was thinking about some eggs, grits, bacon, sausage and toast. I'm hungry as hell."

Just him talking about food made her stomach turn. Before she could say anything, she was back running to the bathroom. Bones shook his head. He wasn't sure what she was gonna do, but he wasn't about to sit in the house with her nasty, sick ass.

Makyla stayed in the bathroom a little longer this time. She felt like death was out to get her. The way she was feeling had her wondering what the fuck was really going on. After cleaning herself up again, she walked into the living room where Bones was chilling at. She swaddled his lap on the couch.

"Man, get your ass away from me."

"Baby, stop acting like that before I go home for real."

"You at home. Fuck you talking about?"

Makyla smiled. She loved when he said that shit. Since they had gotten back together, she did just kind of move in with him. Mike was never at home, and she really didn't have any words for Mehki, so she left them in the dark as to what she had been up to. At the end of the day, she didn't have to say shit to nobody.

"Look, I got some business to handle, so do you need anything before I get ready to leave?"

"No, baby, I should be ok. I'm gonna just go lay down and relax."

Makyla got off his lap then made her way back to the bedroom. Bones got up to take his shower. He needed to go congratulate his team for the nice job they did running up in them hoe ass niggas' spot. Once he was gone, Makyla pulled out her phone so she could call Justice. She had been ignoring her lately, and Makyla wanted to know what was up with her funny acting ass.

After just two rings, Makyla was sent straight to voicemail. *Man, that bitch irritating as fuck."*

Two weeks later… Makyla's birthday

Makyla couldn't believe Justice was still avoiding her calls since that night she met Bones. She hated that after being best friends for so long that Justice could just say fuck her like that. But it was her day and she wasn't about to worry about that shit. She was just happy that both of her brothers called her first thing in the morning to wish her a happy birthday.

She stood in the mirror looking at herself. As she admired her body in the red dress that she was wearing, she couldn't help but to notice that she was picking up some weight. She figured that maybe it was because she was no longer working and just sitting around the house whenever she wasn't at school.

"Damn, I look good," she said to her reflection.

"You sure the fuck do. We might have to say fuck this party and stay in the bed all night."

Makyla bent over and did a lil twerk for him.

"What we gon' do all night boy?"

Bones grinned. "You better stop playing with me before I rip that muthafucka off and have your ass crying for your birthday."

Makyla giggled. As fun as that sounded, she wanted to go party. Bones had made plans for them, and she was ready to go out and party.

For the first time that day, Makyla gave Bones a good look. "Damn, baby, you are looking handsome."

"Shid, you late to the party. I always look good."

"You're so fucking cocky," she said, placing a kiss on his lips.

"Come on, let's go before we end up in this bitch fucking like wild animals."

Makyla didn't even mind that they ended up at their favorite spot. She loved the family members that she did meet and from what she could tell, they all loved her. Most were surprised that they were able to meet anyone that he was involved with. Bones never was the type to have females around. Makyla and Bones were greeted with lots of love. His family even went out their way to decorate the place in all red, white and black.

"Hey, my babies," April cheerfully said, giving them both a hug.

"Hey, ma."

"Hi, Ms. April," Makyla politely said.

"Hey, baby, and happy birthday. You look so beautiful tonight."

"Thank you so much."

One of Bones' auntie walked over to the crowd.

"Here you two go. Let's get the party started," she said, handing over some drinks.

"Hold up, I know it's your birthday, but I know you're not about to drink."

Makyla looked at her then Bones. "Huh? What are you talking about?"

April figured she wasn't playing stupid and really didn't know what was going on. She grabbed Makyla by the hand. "Excuse us, let me go talk to her right quick."

Bones stood there wondering what that was about but watched them walk away. April pulled her daughter-in-law into the restroom.

"What is going on, Ms. April?"

"Girl, are you pregnant?" She quickly asked.

Makyla wasn't trying to be disrespectful, but,

"Hell no!" rushed out of her mouth.

April gave her the side eye. "I think you should just hold up on that drinking tonight and go to the doctor. I'm looking at you, and I have a strong feeling about this."

Makyla laughed it off, but secretly kept what she said in mind. Maybe the lady was on to something.

"Ok, daughter, I guess we can head back to this party of yours."

The ladies walked out of the restroom to find Bones standing there waiting on his baby.

"Damn, what took y'all so long?"

"Nothing, baby, we were talking," Makyla said.

Bones wrapped her up in his arms. "Come talk to this dick," he said, pulling her closer, back towards the restroom.

"Oh, hell nah! Let me get the fuck away from y'all horny muthafuckas!" April yelled.

Both Bones and Makyla laughed. "Damn ma, I was just playing."

They all returned to the party. Makyla couldn't stop thinking about what she was told and couldn't wait to go to the doctor. She just hoped and prayed that Bones would be happy if she was.

Throughout the night, April tried to enjoy herself but found herself watching Makyla like a hulk. That girl could say she wasn't pregnant all she wanted to, but she knew. She now looked back and thought about all those days her son would pop up at her crib just to eat or take a nap. All that sleeping was because of that baby growing inside of Makyla's belly.

During the middle of the party, Bones stepped up on stage. "I just wanna thank everyone for coming out to help celebrate my baby's birthday. Come on up here girl and show my people some love."

Makyla was all smiles as she walked on the stage. She then stood between him and the microphone. "Thank you all for helping me celebrate my birthday. I really appreciate all the love from everyone."

Makyla was ready to walk off the stage when Bones grabbed her. "Where you going? I want you to open up your birthday present."

"Present? You already threw me this party, baby."

Bones laughed as his Uncle walked on stage with a huge pitch-black balloon. As she held on to the string, he dug in his pocket to pull out a pen. "Here baby, pop this bitch."

Makyla had the giggles as she wondered what the hell was in the balloon. The crowd did a countdown for her.

"5, 4, 3, 2, 1!" They all yelled.

Makyla poked the balloon then jumped back. She damn near passed out seeing bundles of money falling all on the stage. She jumped up and down before jumping into his arms. "Thank you, baby. I love you so much."

"This why I told your ass to stop crying over your building. I told you I had you, didn't I?"

"Yes, baby, you did," she said, now crying.

April and Bones helped Makyla pick up all her money. She then followed Bones into the back office.

"Before we go back to the party, I want you to see something," Bones said as he started placing the bundles on the counter.

Makyla eyes got big as she saw that he had given her $45,000 for her business and to get shit started.

"I love you, baby."

"What I tell you about that?" Bones said, laughing.

"I don't care what the hell you are saying, baby. I love the fuck out of you. Ain't nobody ever did anything like this for me. I can't help but to love you."

"You trying to have a nigga head all fucked up and shit."

Bones looked over towards her and could tell that she wanted to cry again. He smiled before giving her a hug. "Don't cry, baby, you look too beautiful to be crying. Now let me put your money up so we can go dance and finish enjoying your party."

The two returned to her party after locking her money in the safe. Soon as they came out, one of his cousins brought them a drink. Makyla took the drink but didn't drink it. Bones necked his then hers. He was trying to get fucked up that night, especially since she was driving them home.

The DJ got on the microphone. "Ok, y'all. I got a special request for this song. I hope you all enjoy it."

To my surprise, the DJ put on The Gap band's *Yearning for Your Love*. The party went wild and just about everyone partnered up to dance. As they danced, they sang along with the music.

"You know what, baby? This is one of my best birthdays ever and I owe it all to you," she whispered in his ear.

"Is that right?"

"Yes, baby, you are the best and I swear I owe you big time."

"So, can I have anything I want?" He asked with a slick look on his face.

"Yes baby, anything."

They continued to dance while Bones rubbed all over Makyla's ass. He knew exactly what he wanted from her. It was nothing that he didn't think that she could handle.

"I know what I want from your spoiled ass."

"What?"

"I just want you to always be honest with me and keep shit real. I hate disloyal ass people. I allowed you to be part of my life, so don't disappoint me."

"Baby, I haven't been disloyal yet and I have no reason to start now. I know you always say don't waste my time on loving a thug like you, but I can't help but to love you."

"Man, I keep telling your ass that I'm not the right one, and I'm not shit to love."

"You say that shit, but you show me something different. Even if I tried to stop loving you, I couldn't. It's too late, baby."

Just as the song was ending, he pulled her in for a kiss. She was hardheaded as fuck, but she was his baby.

Once home, they jumped in the shower, then straight in the bed. Both were tired, but it was all worth it.

As they cuddled in the bed, Bones just had to ask,

"What my mama pulled you in the bathroom for?"

Makyla didn't wanna bring up what she really wanted because she knew how he acted like he didn't care about shit. So, she lied.

"Nothing, baby, you know how she be fooling."

Bones held her in his arms until they both were knocked out.

Mehki & Justice

Mehki knocked on Justice's front door. It had been his first time actually getting out of the car and trying to come in. Lil Man looked out the window and saw his daddy at the door. He hurried and opened the door.

"Daddy, I missed you!" He yelled as he jumped in his daddy's arm.

"I missed you too, but you know better than to open that door. Where your mama at?" Mehki asked as he put his son down.

"Daddy, she in her room but…"

Mehki gave him a confused look. "But what?"

"She so sad, Daddy. All she does is cry all day. Did I do something wrong?"

"Nah, baby. You have been the perfect son."

Mehki didn't like that shit not one bit. He knew they had their problems, but she needed to shake that shit around their son.

"Why don't you do daddy a favor and go back to watching tv. I'm gonna go check on mommy."

Lil Man did as he's told, and Mehki made his way to the bedroom. As he slowly opened the door, he could see Justice's back facing the door. She wasn't sleep 'cause he heard her crying. Not knowing what to say, he quietly took his shoes off then climbed in the bed with her. He pulled her into his arms. That only made her cry harder, but she was happy that he was there.

"Stop crying, Justice. I'm sorry, baby. I should have been here for you and not punishing you even more. I was wrong for that."

A crying Justice rolled over to look him in his eyes. "Baby, I'm so sorry for everything, I swear. It's not your fault. I shouldn't have even gone out that night. I shouldn't have been so jealous of Makyla that I made the decision to leave the club that night with Lamar just to get away from her and her lil boyfriend."

"Her boyfriend? What's that nigga name?"

"His name was Brandon, and he was rude and annoying as hell."

Mehki shook his head, "Yeah, baby sis, always had a problem with picking a guy for her."

He had put in his mind to call her ass and ask her why he had never met the nigga. He had never heard of Brandon before. She was out running the streets with a nigga that he had never heard of.

"So, what now, Mehki?" Justice finally asked. At that point, she didn't care about what was going on with Makyla and her new nigga. She was trying to figure out what was gonna happen with her and Mehki.

"I don't like you being all fucked up around our son. And I damn sure don't want you to ever feel like because I'm in the streets, you have to run out and find somebody else to give you attention to."

"Baby, I know now how stupid that was and I'm sorry. I want us to work and be a family. At this point I'm willing to do whatever to make things go back to how it was between us. I want you to be able to trust me again."

Mehki placed a kiss on Justice's lips. "I got you, ma, and I swear I'm gonna do my best to make our family work."

Justice had tears in her eyes again. "Thanks for forgiving me."

"Truth be told, I couldn't forgive you until them niggasren't on earth anymore."

Justice gave Mehki a kiss 'cause she knew exactly what that had met. Although Mehki was willing to move forward from that whole sex tape bullshit, he decided to wait a minute on that marriage shit.

The two laid in the bed a little while longer just talking about their future. He planned on spending a little more time with her so she would never feel alone and definitely his son.

Justice knew that Mehki must had been tired because he drifted away midsentence while they were talking. She didn't mind, as long as they were back on track. Feeling a little better, she climbed out of the bed to check on her son. She really hadn't been herself and after talking to his dad, she knew that he was feeling like everything was his fault. She wanted him to know that he could never do no wrong.

"How's mommy's lil boy doing?" She asked, taking a seat next to him.

"Curious George movie."

"Oh ok. So, lately mommy wasn't feeling to good, but I'm better now. I just want you to know that nothing was your fault. You are my world. and I want you to know that. I love you, Lil Man."

He gave his mom a tight hug before telling her that he loved her too.

"Ok, now that we got that out the way, what are you in the mood to eat?"

"Pizza!" He yelled with excitement.

Thinking about things, Justice decided that they were gonna go to the market and buy everything that they needed to make some homemade pizzas as a family. Then maybe they could bake some cookies and have a movie night.

She went back in the room to put some clothes on. Right before leaving out again, she gave Mehki a kiss. She was happy to have him again.

Bones

Bones sat back in his chair as he listened to how yet again, his crew ran up in another spot. He was proud of these lil niggas. He felt good knowing that since he had been released, he was the one who put the fire under them niggas' asses to expand their business.

"I'm proud of you lil niggas. I told y'all before, never be scared of a muthafucka that bleed just like y'all do. You gotta boss up on these niggas and let them know that you ain't scared of shit."

Although he was in prison and Gunna and Choppa had been running shit, he could tell that those young niggas really looked up to him. He just prayed that they never tried to cross him and have to have their moms burying their asses.

"Man Bones, that shit was live as fuck. They never knew what hit them. And ole' boy in the back had a chance to run or blast at us back. Stupid muthafucka froze up," Lil Ant said, full of excitement.

Bones couldn't help but to laugh. "Ok, I see I have some shooters over here. Once we take over everything, I'm gonna give y'all niggas a lil bonus. Y'all deserve it."

It wasn't long before Bones left to go check on his ole' lady. As he pulled up in front of her house, he was surprised to see Makyla's car in the driveway. Smelling the grill going, he went straight to the backyard.

Makyla was sitting at the table eating a fruit salad and doing her homework. He smiled seeing that she got along with his mom. She was the only person that he really had. He also loved how no matter what, Makyla kept her head in the books, and she was a good girl.

He walked over towards the table. "Hey, baby. Fuck you doing over here?" He asked as he gave her a kiss.

Makyla closed her book then looked up. "I had to leave school a little early today and your mom just so happened to call me to see if I wanted to chill with her for a while."

"Where she at now?"

"In the house making some iced tea for us."

Bones was gonna go check on his mom, but Makyla's beauty had him caught up in a trance. He ended up taking a seat right next to her. "You know you're so fucking beautiful?"

"Yes, and thank you, baby. I think you match my fly," she jokingly said.

April walked out with a pitcher of iced tea. "Hey, baby. Why you over here interrupting our girls' session. I just want to chill with my daughter-in-law and eat some burgers off the grill."

"Man, she mine. I can be where ever she at."

All three of them started to laugh. Bones was always joking around when he wasn't acting so fucking evil.

"I guess since your ass here, you can go flip those burgers over there," April ordered.

"Bullshit, I came to eat not cook shit."

"Baby, please? I'm so hungry," Makyla softly said while rubbing his hand.

Just like you would have guessed, Bones jumped right up to go check on the food. April couldn't help but to laugh. Her son could act like he wasn't in love, but she knew Makyla had him wrapped around her fingers.

"Look, I think you need to tell Bones about what's going on. Soon, it'll all be out."

"No, I'm not ready for that. And truthfully, I'm not sure how he would feel about this situation."

"My son acts all tough and shit, but he really does love you. Tell that boy about that baby or I will," April threatened.

Makyla wasn't ready. She didn't understand just how scared she was to talk to him.

"Please don't say nothing. Just let me tell him on my own please."

"Tell him today and get it out the way, Makyla. That's my son, and I don't play those games. Tell him or I'm saying something my muthafucking self."

Bones walked back over towards the table and took his seat. He looked over towards Makyla and could tell something was wrong with her. For one, it looked like there were tears in her eyes.

"Fuck wrong with you?"

Makyla looked up at Bones, but the truth couldn't come out. "Nothing, I just don't feel too good." She jumped up and grabbed her stuff so she could leave.

Bones looked at his mom. "What the fuck happened?"

"Go talk to that girl."

Bones got up to follow behind Makyla, but she was long gone. Just that fast, she had dipped. Bones went back to the backyard to say bye to his mom.

"Aye ma, she must've left. I'm about to go find her and see what's going on."

April wanted to say something so bad. Now thinking over the way Makyla reacted, she felt somewhat bad for applying pressure on her. Maybe she should have just let her handle her own business.

"Ok then, call me later."

Bones left to go try to find his baby. He hated when something was wrong with her and he didn't know how to fix shit. He didn't know where else she could be at besides his crib. He couldn't help but to speed thru traffic trying to get home and see what the fuck her problem was.

Once he made it home and did a walk thru, he saw that Makyla was nowhere around. Flopping down on the couch, he pulled out his phone then called her ass. After getting no answer, he called her three more times before giving up.

CHAPTER 8

MEHKI

Mehki had been staying at Justice's house, but after having two more of his spots ran up in, he knew it was time for his feet to hit the streets again. He needed to figure out who the fuck been shitting on him and his crew lately. In the matter of a month, four spots had been run in and he had lost a few members of his crew. After grabbing a water bottle out the fridge, Mehki took a seat on the couch. It didn't take long for his phone to start going off.

"What's up, Bro?"

"Man, you ain't gon' believe this shit.," Mike calmly said.

Now sitting up, fully alarmed, "What's up, Bro, spit that shit out."

Mike hesitated to say anything at first, only 'cause he knew that Mehki was gonna be hurt behind the situation.

"Mike, stop acting like a pussy and talk!" Mehki yelled into the phone.

"I was on the block checking on everything, making sure shit was good, right? Well, some niggas ran up in that bitch, but me and BJ were able to dip out the back door and hit the fence. Man, these niggas not playing and they comin' fully loaded. Won't no point in trying to have a shoot out with these niggas. We weren't gonna walk out that bitch alive."

"Man bro, I'm just glad you alive right now. Makyla would kill me if anything ever happened to you."

"So, that nigga BJ said he got a look at one of the niggas and knows exactly who that nigga is. What's the plan, bro?" Mike asked, ready to catch another body.

"I'm gonna scoop you later, bro. I want your ass to stay low for a minute and don't worry about shit. Whoever tried to kill you will be dead before the fucking week is over. I put that on myself, nigga."

"Alright, bro, I'll see you later."

"Love you, bro."

Before hanging up the phone, Mike told his big bro that he loved him too.

***

Mehki was woken by the smell of food cooking and for a moment, he forgot that he was at home. He got up and made his way into the kitchen to find Makyla standing there cooking.

"So, your ass do know where you live?" He asked, taking a seat at the island.

"I've been home for a few days now. It looks like y'all don't know where y'all live. Ain't nobody been here with me," Makyla said, stirring up a pot of spaghetti.

"I know where me and Mike been. Where the fuck you been staying?"

"I've been with a friend. Not that it's any of your business," she said, giving off much attitude.

"So, who is this nigga you been running around with?"

"Mehki, get out my business. I'm grown as hell and can do as I please."

"You so fucking stubborn and it don't make any sense. You know how I get down in these streets. I was just trying to make sure you weren't fucking around with a nigga I got beef with."

Makyla quickly yelled out, "I'm not!"

"I know you're grown, but you still my lil sister, and I have every right to be worried about you. I wouldn't know what to do if somebody hurt you just because of my bullshit."

Hearing him say that took away her attitude. It wasn't something new because he always told her and Mike that, but lately, she been in her own little world. Seeing his sister cry made Mehki hurry to be by her side. He hugged on to her tight and allowed her to cry on his chest.

"It's ok, sis. No matter what, I love you and won't shit ever change about that," Mehki said, showing his sister some love.

"I'm so sorry for being such a bitch lately, Mehki!" She cried out.

"It's ok, sis. Just let a nigga get a plate of food," he said, causing her to start laughing.

It wasn't long before they both were sitting at the table eating and just talking about random shit. It felt like so much time had passed since the last time they were able to be around each other with having an attitude. All that was missing was Mike.

"So, since you've been at Justice's house, has she told you how she's been ignoring me ad shit. That funny acting bitch ain't even call me on my birthday."

Mehki, shook his head. Makyla had no idea what the fuck Justice had been through. "Aye sis, before you get all rowdy, maybe you need to talk to her and see what's going on. She might be in a fucked-up space right now."

Makyla could tell that he knew something and wasn't telling her. "What's going on with her, Mehki? I can tell you know something."

Mehki paused for a moment, he really didn't wat to talk about it. "Look, I'll take care of the kitchen. Ride over there and talk to your girl. Y'all my heart and I can't have y'all beefing or whatever you wanna call it."

Makyla got up so she could get dressed. Maybe she was over reacting and needed to talk to best friend.

Justice & Makyla

Makyla stood on the porch waiting for Justice to open the door for her. She had missed her and her nephew so much. Justice looked out the opened the door. She knew that she had been playing Makyla to the left and deep down inside, she couldn't blame Makyla for the bullshit that happened to her. That was all on her being stupid. It was crazy how she saw Makyla happy and let jealousy take over and cloud her mind that night. It was just like Mehki said, all she had to do was sit her ass down and wait her turn.

As she stood in the doorway, her and Makyla just stared at each other. In the matter of seconds, the two friends fell into each other's arms. They both allowed their tears to fall.

"I'm so sorry, Makyla. I missed you so much," Justice cried out.

Once they finally pulled away from each other, Justice stood to the side so Makyla could step in.

"Where's my nephew at?"

"Girl, me and Mehki took him to the bounce house and he played all day. Soon as he came home, he collapsed in his room."

They both laughed.

"Look, I'm pretty sure we need to talk, so let's have a seat."

"I have been calling you like crazy. Today, I finally asked Mehki what the hell was your problem, but then he told me to calm down and just come talk to you. You know he hates when we fall out, especially when it's over some bullshit that could easily be talked out."

"You're right, Makyla."

"Ok, so what happened?" Makyla finally asked.

"Girl, so much. That night I was on some bullshit and ended up leaving the club with some nigga named Lamar that we went to school with."

Makyla cut her off. "Really bitch?"

Justice gave her the side eye. "Let me finish. Anyways, we went back to his place and fucked. I was so stupid that I let this nigga blindfold me and tie me down to the headboard."

"Oh, so you were single single that night.?"

Tears came to Justice's eyes. She didn't want to repeat this story, but her best friend deserved to know what had happened.

"What's wrong, Justice?" Makyla asked, seeing that she wasn't no longer in a joking mood.

"Girl, Mehki came over here tripping and at first I was talking shit until he threw his phone in my face. Tell me why Lamar recorded us fucking?"

"What the fuck! Are you fucking serious?"

"That's not it," she whispered as her tears began to roll.

Makyla could tell it was something serious. She got up from her favorite spot on the love seat, then made her way over to the couch were her friend was sitting now.

"Justice, talk to me, boo. What happened?"

"He recorded me getting fucked by him and his friend. I must be the stupidest bitch on earth. I was so happy to be doing me that I didn't even notice that I was sucking and fucking on two different niggas."

Makyla felt bad for her friend and soon, she was holding her and crying right along with her.

"Oh, my gawd, Justice! I'm so sorry that happened to you. That shit wasn't right at all."

"Girl, your brother went the fuck off. And for a while, he wouldn't even talk to me. Believe it or not, I was more hurt about not having him in my life than what happened."

"Damn, Justice, I feel so bad. I was so caught up in Brandon that I didn't even see who you left with. I suck at being a friend."

Justice giggled, "Nah boo, I wouldn't say all that. I still love your ass."

"I love you too, girl."

"Enough of that crying. Girl, I'm so glad that Mehki forgave me and now we're able to move on as a family."

Makyla smiled, "I'm so happy for you two."

Makyla felt her phone vibrate, then pulled it out her back pocket. She shook her head as she saw that it was

Bones. It had been a minute since she ran away from him at his mom's house. Truthfully, she was scared to talk to him. Since she didn't answer, he left her a text.

Brandon: I'm tired of playing games with your lil' ass. Call me right fucking now or we gonna have a problem. And whatever nigga you been with about to die.

Makyla was scared and quickly texted back.

Makyla: Ok, Brandon, but I wasn't with no other nigga.

"Justice, it was great talking to you again and I'm sorry for not being there for you, but I have to go handle something right quick."

"Ok, boo. Maybe we can get together for lunch one day soon," Justice suggested.

"Sounds like a plan," Makyla cheerfully said before walking out of the door.

Once in the car, she hurried to call her crazy ass thug.

Bones and Makyla

Bones answered on the first ring, so she'd know he wasn't playing with her ass.

"Hey, baby," she softly said into the phone.

"Fuck all that shit, where the fuck you been?" he questioned.

"At home, baby."

Bones wanted to hurt her, but all that baby shit had him like putty in her hands. "Look, I'm about to text you an address. Hurry up and pull up."

She didn't get a chance to respond because he quickly hung up the phone. She pulled off from Justice's house wondering if she should go. Just as she was thinking about going home, Bones texted her again.

Bones: You got 5 fucking minutes muthafucka

Just off his behavior, she knew not to fuck with him, so she looked at the address one last time before heading that way. She prayed his mom didn't say shit to him, and she could get him to calm down before talking about the baby. Now thinking back on things, she wished that she would have just said something instead of hiding from him.

It took her a whole ten minutes to get to the location. It was an abandoned building. Well, it was a store front. "Oh, hell nah!" She mumbled to herself. Now she was really having doubts of getting out.

Just as she was thinking about pulling off, Bones snatched the car door open. "Get the fuck out."

Makyla slowly got out of the car. "Hey, baby."

"Why a nigga gotta chase your ass and shit? What the fuck going on with you?" He yelled.

Makyla could see that his fist was balled while he yelled and knew that he was pissed.

"Calm down, baby, you're scaring me."

Seeing that she was really scared, he tried to calm down. He pulled her up in his arms for a hug. "I wasn't trying to scare you, bae. I was just worried about your ass. Man, where the fuck you been?"

"Baby, I've been at home. I just needed some time to get myself together."

Bones gave her a strange look. "You fuckin' somebody else?"

"No, stupid ass. Just because I wasn't up under you that don't mean I was out being a hoe. Don't ever ask me no shit like that no more," Makyla blurted out with so much attitude.

"Man, calm your ass down. I just needed to know that you still down for a nigga, that's it, muthafucka."

Makyla placed her hands over his, seeing if he would calm down himself. "You know I love your crazy ass and ain't trying to be with no lame ass nigga."

Bones now had a little smirk on his face. "And that's the way it better be. I'll have to bury a nigga over your ass."

Makyla laughed before getting serious. "So why are we here?"

"Didn't I tell your ass that we needed to start looking for you a store? Come take a look inside and see if you could fuck with this one. The realtor already in there waiting on your slow ass."

"Baby, you serious?"

"I was serious when I gave you the money for this bitch. Now come on before this man think I was on some bullshit."

Makyla allowed Bones to lead her into the building. Soon as she walked in, she fell in love with the place. Her imagination took over, and she could picture everything clean and set up.

"Oh, my gawd! This place is beautiful, baby. Plus, it's in a great location. I could see business booming here."

The realtor butted into their conversation. "See, I told you that your wife would love this place. I knew what I was talking about."

Bones looked over at Makyla as she looked around some more. "Makyla, so what do you think? Do you want this muthafucka or do you wanna look at a few more places?"

"I love this one, baby."

"You sure? I mean, it is your bread. I just want your first choice to be your best."

Makyla walked towards Bones. After placing a kiss on his lips, she shook her head yes.

"This is the place, baby."

Bones turned his attention towards Mr. Jones. "I guess she gon' take this building."

***

It took a minute, but Makyla was now the owner of her own business. She couldn't wait to finalize everything and get her name on the building. As they walked back to her car, she couldn't help but to keep thanking Bones for looking out for her.

"I swear this is the nicest thing that anyone has done for me."

"Yeah, yeah, tell me anything," he said, leaning against her car.

She stepped in his face. "I love your cocky ass."

"You so fucking hardheaded. I told you not to waste your love on a nigga like me. I ain't shit."

Makyla laughed like always. "But you make it so hard not to."

"So, what you about to get into?" He asked.

With her body pressed up against his, she whispered, "I just wanna be up under you, baby. I really missed you."

Bones smiled, feeling her little hand rubbing on his dick. He could tell that she really did miss him. "Your ass don't miss me. Your freaky ass just miss this dick. Follow daddy so you can get what you want."

Bones opened the door to let her get in. He was about to straight up punish her ass and give her a lesson on making him have to go find her ass.

CHAPTER 9

MEHKI & MIKE

"Are you sure the nigga name Gunna who ran up in my shit?" Mehki asked BJ.

"Hell yeah, nigga. That nigga family stay around the corner from my grandma, and we use to play ball back in the day."

Mehki sat there soaking up what BJ was saying. He was ready to go pay Gunna a visit.

"Aye, bro, let's ride out and find this nigga," Mike quickly said.

His first kill made him sick, but he was pretty sure that the second one wouldn't have. He was ready to ride out.

Mehki gave BJ a look. "You riding or sliding, lil nigga?"

"Aye, I'm young, but never a bitch. Plus, I done put in work before. I'm ready," BJ excitedly said.

They all climbed into Mehki's car and listened as BJ gave them directions to the other side of Detroit. Mehki didn't fuck with that side, but he didn't mind taking that ride to catch a body.

After bending a few corners, BJ finally announced that they were on the block. Mehki killed his engine as he looked over their surroundings.

"You see that house right there with the pretty flowers, that's his grandma's house. When he ain't in the streets, he be over here laying low."

Mehki sat there for a good ten minutes before starting the car back up and pulling off.

"Fuck you doing, bro?"

"Chill the fuck out, Mike. I got this."

Mike didn't say shit else. He knew that if his bro said he had shit under control, that's what the fuck was going on. Mehki drove until he ended up at a gas station. He put $20 in the tank and grabbed some wraps. It was gonna be a long night, and he needed to smoke. Just as he was stepping out, a nigga walking in bumped into him. He instantly got pissed seeing that the nigga wasn't gonna acknowledge that he had bumped him.

"Excuse you, nigga," Mehki spit out.

"Fuck you, nigga. Fuck I look like apologizing to a hoe ass nigga!" Gunna barked.

Before Mehki could respond, the little bitch that Gunna was with spoke up. "Gunna, come on, baby. We don't need all this bullshit tonight."

"Yeah, Gunna, you better listen to your lil bitch. These not the problems you want tonight," Mehki teased.

"Man, who the fuck you talking to, my nigga? You must not know who I am."

Mehki was nowhere near scared and he laughed in Gunna's face. "You right, Gunna. I don't know your bitch ass."

Gunna was pissed off as his girl pulled him in the gas station. He hated not being able to do anything because she was with him. But he promised himself that if he ever saw him again that he was killing him on sight. He watched as Mehki hoped in his car.

Mehki wasn't no fool and knew soon as he heard the bitch say Gunna that it was the nigga that he was looking for. "Aye, BJ, you saw that nigga I was just talking to?"

"Yeah, did you see bro with the gun out the window waiting on that nigga to jump stupid? That was that nigga," he announced, too excited.

"Yeah, I'm hip. I'm glad y'all niggas didn't get out acting a fool. We about to follow him away from the gas station and all these fucking cameras. It's a wrap for that nigga and fuck that bitch he with."

Mike finally took his eyes from the direction of Gunna's car. "Let's go. That nigga just got back in his car."

Although Mehki followed Gunna, he made sure to keep his distance so it wouldn't be obvious.

"Bro, I know we ain't just gonna keep following this bitch. Pull up on the side of his car and let me and BJ handle this nigga!" Mike yelled.

"Whoa! Baby, that's the shit I'm talking about!" Mehki yelled out as he sped up a little to be side by side with Gunna's car.

BJ was sitting behind Mehki but quickly slid over to be behind Mike. Before they could ask him if he was ready, the nigga was already pulling out his piece. Mehki got closer towards the car.

Mike didn't give a fuck. Soon as Gunna saw them right on his shit, Mike was blasting rounds in his car. BJ wasn't a hoe either, he was putting in work. Gunna soon lost control of his car and Mehki pushed down on the gas, leaving his car to flip over.

"Yes, baby! Yes! I love that wild shit. I'm proud of you niggas!" Mehki yelled as he quickly got away from the incident.

As he pulled up to BJ mama's crib, he gave him a dap. "Lil nigga, you got heart and I love that shit. It's late but I'll be around here first thing in the morning to fill those pockets."

"Ok, bro. that's cool with me."

As he began to walk towards the house, Mike yelled out. "Aye, nigga, lay low for a minute and be cool."

"Ok, bro!" BJ yelled back.

Mehki calmed down a little to kick it with his bro. Plus, he wanted to make sure he was alright. He could remember the last time his bro killed a muthafucka, he damn near lost his mind.

"You good, bro?"

"Hell yeah. It was easier this time. Now I just wanna go lay up under Roni."

"Look at this shit, lil bro in love and shit. That's cool and all, just make sure you keep her out this street shit. You know us thugs don't give a fuck about shit when it's time to kill," Mehki said, dropping knowledge.

"You right, man. Plus, she pregnant. I wouldn't know what to do if something happened to them. I'll probably go crazy."

"Damn nigga, so I'm about to be a fucking uncle?"

"Hell yeah, bro. I wanted to tell you earlier, but I didn't know how to let that shit out," Mike admitted.

"It's cool, bro. Congratulations, my baby."

They finally had made it to Roni's crib. "Alright, bro, you be safe out here," Mike said before getting out the car.

"You too, nigga. These streets are hot!" Mehki yelled out the window before driving off.

Mike went in to be with his baby. Roni was doing what she did best nowadays. She was in the bed knocked out sleep. He undressed then climbed in the bed with her. After that wild ass night, he just needed to chill with his girl.

Mehki thought about going home, but after driving by the crib and seeing that Makyla wasn't even there, he went straight to Justice's house. He really didn't feel like being alone.

Mehki called Justice soon as he hit her block.

"Aye, baby, open up the garage for me."

"Dang, Mehki, I just got out the shower. Let me throw something on right quick!" Justice hollered over the phone.

As Mehki pulled up in the driveway, he saw that she had on some tight ass pants and t- shirt. He sat there for a minute and admired her beauty and shape. He loved that girl. After pulling up in the garage and killing the engine, they went into the house.

"You hungry, baby?" Justice asked as soon as they walked into the house.

"Hell yeah, but not for no real food."

Justice couldn't help but to laugh. "Boy you so fucking nasty."

"While I go hope in the shower, you can go in the room and take that shit off. I miss hitting that shit," he admitted.

"Ok, baby. Just hurry up," she said as she walked towards her bedroom.

Mehki really did miss making love to his baby mama and tonight, she was gonna know just how much. Mehki's plans were to fuck the shit out of her that night, but once out of the shower, he grabbed his clothes. He could feel the engagement ring that he had brought for Justice. He smiled, feeling that tingly feeling that was telling him to go ahead and man up.

He climbed in the bed, but instead of positioning himself on top of her, he cuddled up on the side of her naked body.

"You know I love the fuck out of you, right?"

"Yes, Mehki, and I love you just as much, if not more," she admitted as she turned his way.

Mehki held out the small black box and before he could ask, Justice was already crying and screaming yes.

"Oh my gawd! Baby, yes! Yes, I will marry you!" She screamed, damn near falling out the bed.

Now sitting up, Mehki grabbed her arm. "Calm down, baby, and let me do this the right way."

As he started to ask if she would marry him, he couldn't even get it all the way out because she kept screaming and waving her hand in his face.

"Bae, calm down so I can put your ring on!" He hollered.

After a few more seconds, she finally stopped jumping around and took a seat back on the bed. She was all smiles as he slid the ring on her finger. This was the day that she had been waiting for. Once she was done crying and admiring her ring, the two made sweet passionate love. Mehki had made up his mind that it was time to leave these streets alone and be the family man that Justice and his son needed in their life.

Bones

The sound of his phone constantly ringing woke Bones straight out of his sleep. He tried to sit up but couldn't because Makyla was knocked out on him. After beating them cheeks all night and early morning, he wasn't expecting her to wake up any time soon.

He slid out the bed to grab his phone. It fucked him up to see that he had twelve miss calls. He knew if he had of told niggas where he stayed, he would have a house full.

Since Choppa had been the last call and the muthafucka that called him the most, he called him back first.

"What's up, bro? What's the word?"

Clearly upset and emotional, Choppa told Bones the news. "Boy, I got some bad news."

Bones could tell by his shaky voice that it was something serious. He took a seat back on the bed.

"What's up, bro?"

"Man, it's Gunna. Him and Gina were killed last night."

"Man, what the fuck! Bro, tell me you lying. What the fuck happened, my nigga?" Bones yelled, causing Makyla to lift her head up.

"Baby, what's wrong?" She mumbled, clearly still half sleep.

Bones didn't bother to answer. He held the phone to his ear as Choppa told him what he heard happened to their childhood friend.

"So, do y'all niggas know who the fuck did this shit?" Bones finally asked.

It was hard trying to be strong behind Gunna's death. That nigga had been his friend since fucking diapers.

"Nah, not now, but I got the young boys out listening to the streets right now," Choppa sadly told him.

"Alright, man, just let me know if anybody hear anything. I'm gonna go see his mom later and make sure she good," Bones said before hanging up.

Makyla sat up then leaned over his back. She placed a kiss on the side of his face. "Baby, are you ok?"

"My muthafucking bro was killed last night," Bones said, putting his head down.

Makyla wrapped her arms around him. "Baby, I'm so sorry to hear that. Is there anything I can do?"

"Nah, baby."

Bones leaned back on the headboard. He was hurt, but the thug in him wouldn't let him shed a tear about losing his childhood friend. Although he played that tough role, Makyla could tell that he was hurt. She didn't say anything as she just held onto him. Once he pulled her closer onto his chest, she knew he needed her to be there for him.

"It's ok, baby. You can let your true feelings out around me."

"I'm good, Makyla. That was my fucking nigga man, and I can't believe somebody killed him. He didn't deserve no shit like this."

"Was he having problems with anyone that you know of?" She questioned.

"Hell nah, not that I can think of. Just know whoever did this shit is gonna feel my pain. I'm gonna do them niggas dirty."

Not knowing what to say, Makyla lifted her head then placed a kiss on his lips. "Ok, baby. It'll all be alright, Brandon."

***

Makyla woke back up to Bones still sleep, his head resting on her breast. He also still had his arms wrapped around her. She didn't wanna wake him up so for a while she softly rubbed the back of his head. She hated that some crazy ass fool killed his friend. She secretly prayed that if he did go out looking for revenge, he made it back home to her.

"You playin' in my hair, I guess you volunteering to fix my shit later."

"Yes, baby, whatever you want. I got you. You want me to make you some breakfast?"

Sitting up, Bones declined her offer. "Nah, I'm really not hungry. I need to get dressed and go see Gunna's Mom."

"Ok, baby. I'm gonna wash your clothes before I go to class. Once I'm out, I'll check on you to see how you're doing."

"When you get out of class, just meet me at my mom's crib. I have to stop over there later anyways."

Makyla wasn't too happy to go to his mom's house and he saw that on her face. He wasn't sure what happened the last time they were all at his mom's house, but he didn't feel like getting in all that bullshit. Maybe later he'll talk to the both of them together. He couldn't have his girls not fucking with one another.

The two finally climb out of the bed to join each other in the shower. Makyla was happy that she wasn't really showing because of the way he was all on her. But she knew it was only a matter of time before she would have to say something. All they did was have wild, crazy sex whenever they were together, so really it shouldn't surprise him whenever she did tell him about the baby.

"Makyla, don't forget to go to my mom's when you get out of class," Bones reminded her as he got ready to make his way to Gunna's mom house.

"Baby, I'm not. And you be careful out there."

"Fuck you talking about? I'm always careful," he snapped back.

Now standing face to face with her love, Makyla held on to his hands. "Brandon, you don't always have to have your guard up with me. It's ok to express your feelings and show emotions, baby. I can look into your eyes and tell that you're hurt and want somebody to pay for hurting you. I might not be into all that thug life, killing and shit, but I love you and have your back on whatever."

Bones gave her a kiss on her full juicy lips. "Just call me when you get to my mom's. I'll see you later, baby." Just like that, he was walking out the door.

Makyla stood there stuck. She hated how he was, but only because she knew that he did care about her. What niggas were out here buying a bitch whatever she wanted or needed? Then he cashed out on her building. That itself was a sign that he cared about her future. On top of that, he stayed up under her, so she knew he wasn't dealing with another bitch on the side.

Just like she said, before she left for class, she made sure to do his laundry. She had just folded and put his shit away when she saw that she had less than fifteen minutes to get to class. She hurried out the door. Finals were just around the corner and she didn't wanna be late.

***

Bones pulled up to Gunna's mom's house and just as he thought, it was only about two cars parked out front. It was crazy how people claimed to love you all while you are alive, but when you die, nobody really gives a fuck.

Climbing out of the car to pay his respects was gonna be the hardest thing ever since his grandma had died. Gunna's mom, Mrs. Evans, was always like a second mom to him. As he walked in the door, Mrs. Evans sat on

177

the couch crying her eyes out. This was the second son that she had lost to the streets.

Seeing Bones, she jumped up from the couch and fell straight into his arms. "They done killed my baby!" She cried out.

"I know ma, but I'm gonna handle it for you. I promise, I'll get the muthafucka for you." He whispered in her ear.

Gunna's dad sat in the chair in the corner of the living room. Even though there were a few family members there, he was in his own little world. Him and his wife had just lost their last child to dumb shit, and he was hurt. All their lives he had kept a job as a janitor at the neighborhood school. He tried to show his boys that it was more to life than running the streets and selling drugs. Now they both were dead 'cause they didn't wanna listen. He knew Bones his whole life and still didn't care too much for him. He knew he wasn't shit either.

Mrs. Evans, her sister, Sabrina, and Bones sat around just a little longer talking about the funeral arrangements. Mr. Evans sat there listening but didn't say a word. He really didn't give a fuck.

"Ma, I gotta get up from out of here, but here, take care of my bro's arrangements. Just keep me posted on everything."

Bones had to get the fuck from out that house. All that crying on top of Mr. Evans looking at him as if shit was all his fault, he would have hated to explode and hurt that man.

Bones' next stop was the block. Somebody knew something, and he was about to find out who killed his nigga.

Makyla

Leaving her class for the day, Makyla rubbed her stomach as it growled. She was hungry as hell and needed to eat. Once in the car, she pulled out her phone to call Bones since he wanted her to do so.

"Hey baby. How are you feeling?" She said into the phone when he answered after the third ring.

"Hey. You just got out of class?"

"Yes, and I'm so hungry. I was gonna stop by this chicken spot and get some food. Do you want something?"

"I'm hungry, but you know better than to walk into my mom's house with some outside food. She will go crazy. Plus, I know she's cooking right now. Head over there, I'm on my way."

Hearing April was already cooking up some shit, Makyla was all smiles. She couldn't wait to get there even though the last time they were there she had pissed her off.

"Alright, baby, see you there. And you be careful."

Before hanging up, Bones said, "Alright."

Makyla made it to April's house in no time and quickly rushed to the porch. After ringing the bell, she waited patiently for her to answer.

"Hey, Ms. April."

"Hey, baby. I'm glad my baby found you. I got tired of him asking me what the hell happened between us, but don't worry, I didn't tell him anything."

Makyla laughed, "I'm not trying to be funny, but Brandon said you were cooking, so can I come in and eat. We can talk over food."

April started laughing herself. She didn't even notice that she had blocked her daughter-in-law from entering the house.

"My bad, come on, baby."

The two ladies went into the house and while Makyla washed her hands, April made their plates.

"I wanna say thank you for not telling Bones about the baby. I know I need to say something, but sometimes he can be so empty."

"Empty? Girl, what are you talking about?" April asked, confused as hell.

"It's just that sometimes he can be so sweet towards me, but his feelings are never there. It's like he treats me like he cares, but if I tell him I care, he tells me not to. Why does he do that?"

"My son has this problem where he thinks if he shows feelings, that means he's a hoe. He thinks it's gonna take away from his street credit. I tell him all the time to treat you right before he loses you. Maybe this baby will change him and make him realize that it's ok to show love."

"I have a doctor's appointment in two days and I'm kind of nervous. Can you go with me, then we can plan out the best way to tell your big baby the good news?"

April couldn't help but to be excited. She always wanted a grandchild. "I would love that, Makyla. I'm just happy that it's only two days away. I can't wait to see my grandbaby."

They continued to eat and talk about whatever came to mind. It wasn't long before the man of the day walked into the house.

"What's up, ma?"

"Hey, baby. Go ahead and wash your hands, so I can make your plate." Before going to wash his hands, he went over towards Makyla and gave her a kiss.

"Hey, baby, you alright?"

"Yeah, I just needed to eat," Makyla admitted.

Bones took a seat at the table after cleaning up. He couldn't help but to watch Makyla smash. He thought it was cute that she wasn't scared to eat around a nigga. She was real at all times.

"Here goes your plate," April said, setting his plate down on the table.

April took her seat back at the table and couldn't help but to just stare at her son. "You know, Bones, I'm so sorry to hear about your friend Gunna. I knew how close you two were."

Bones swallowed his food. "It's all good, ma. Everything gon' be alright." Within the same breath, Bones was back eating his food like wasn't shit wrong, and he didn't just lose a close friend.

Makyla gave April a look, trying to see if she noticed how empty he was. She shook her head but didn't say anything to her son. She was used to him acting like that but wish he didn't. Because April had cooked such a good meal like every time they came over, Makyla took it upon herself to clean the kitchen. While she stayed in the kitchen, April and her son went to go talk in the living room.

"You know, Bones, I really like Makyla. I really believe that she is the right one for you."

"Ma, what I tell you about all that shit? Every time I'm over here, you bringing this up."

"Boy, fuck what you talkin' about. The only reason she still around after all this time is because you love that girl."

Bones shook his head. He hated how she always want to talk about the same shit every time she saw him.

"Ma, chill for me please," he begged.

"Ok, just one more thing. So, if she decided to stop fucking with you right now and next week, she with a whole other nigga that's gonna show her his true feelings, what you gon' do? How would you feel?"

Bones laughed, "First of all, she ain't fucking stupid and if a nigga even thinks they gon' get her, I'm gonna kill him."

April was now laughing at her son. "Boy, you bat shit crazy with no title over that girl. You don't own her, and you can't make her stay with your crazy ass. You better get your shit together before a nigga that ain't gon' put the streets before her come along."

Just then, Makyla walked into the room. "I'm done with the kitchen and sleepy now."

"You ready to roll out, Makyla?" Bones asked.

"Yeah, I'm ready to go to bed."

Makyla mad sure to give April a tight hug before they left. She really did care about her.

After a long, hot shower, Bones and Makyla cuddled in the bed, just holding each other like any other night. The only difference was that he was stuck wide awake thinking about the shit his mom was talking about. She did make a point. He had to be feeling some type of way about Makyla if it crossed his mind to kill a nigga if she ever moved on. Then he thought about Marcus. All this time, he had put in his mind that he killed him for being a hoe ass nigga with too much mouth, but it could have been because he was trying to pull Makyla away from him. Just thinking over shit made him look over at his girl and place a kiss on her forehead. "

What the fuck did you do to me girl?" He mumbled to himself.

CHAPTER 10
MAKAYLA

Makyla pulled up to April's house extra early. Today was her doctor's appointment and they both were excited to see the baby. April walked out of the house wearing a huge smile on her face. Most women didn't respond too well with being a grandma, but she was acting like she had won the lottery. He son had finally gave her what she's been begging for and now that she thought about it, she was happy that he waited for the right woman to come around. She wasn't sure how shit would have worked out if he would have gotten one of those thots that he fucked with pregnant.

"Hey, baby! You ready to go check on my grandbaby?" April asked, as she put on her seatbelt.

"Yeah, I'm ready. I just can't wait to tell Brandon. I have a feeling that he will be happy because lately, he's been trying to slowly open up to me," Makyla admitted.

April smiled knowing that her little talk with her son worked. She knew if he thought about somebody else with her, he would have got his act together.

Once at the clinic, Makyla was happy that she didn't have to wait too long before being called. Her and April followed the nurse to the back. Soon, she was laying on the table with cold gel on her stomach. Since she wasn't that far along, there wasn't much to see, but she still smiled at what her and Bones made. Even April was in tears seeing the baby on the monitor.

"Ok, Makyla, everything is looking good at this point. Looking over everything, I can say that you're at eleven weeks now. I would like to set up another appointment in two weeks so we can monitor the baby's growth," Dr. Ross said, wiping her belly clean.

"So, everything looking good?" April butted in to ask.

"Yeah, ma'am, for both mom and baby."

Walking out the clinic, Makyla was surprised to see her baby brother and his girlfriend, Roni, walking in.

"What y'all doing here?" Makyla asked.

"Hey, sis," Roni said, wearing a big smile on her face.

Mike was smiling as well. "Man, I can ask you the same damn thing," he said, giving her a strange look.

They all laughed because they were all there for the same reason.

"So, how far along are you, Makyla?" Roni asked.

"I'm only eleven weeks."

Mike didn't say too much. He was still trying to wrap her head around the fact that his sister was pregnant right along with his girl. It was crazy how shit worked.

"I'm gonna let you guys go before y'all be late for the appointment, but how about we all get together later this week for dinner. We haven't done that in a while and we all need to catch up," Makyla suggested.

"Hell yeah, we need that. I'll call bro later once we leave from out of here," Mike announced.

After everyone said their goodbyes and passed out hugs. Makyla looked up to see that April had pulled up with her car.

"Come on, baby, we got some stuff to get from the store!" April yelled out the window.

***

After leaving the doctor's, April and Makyla put things in motion. They had everything planned out for Bones' surprise. The first step was to the dollar store. They purchased a bunch of balloons and a picture frame for the ultrasound picture. Before paying for everything, Makyla grabbed a white teddy bear that held onto a red heart that said *I Love You* on it. Everything was gonna be perfect.

Making it back to Bones' condo, April rushed to start cooking her son's favorite meal. Today was his day and she wanted him to feel like a fucking king.

"Ok, Ms. April, I set everything up for him. It's so pretty, I can't wait to see his face."

"Girl, I haven't seen him in his feelings since his grandma died. He didn't even express his feelings when his dad walked out on us, but I got a feeling this will do it."

"You think so?" Makyla questioned.

"Hell yeah. I don't know what type of voodoo you did on my son, but you're the one and I've been telling him that before I even met you."

Makyla looked down at her ringing phone. "Hold on, let me answer this."

"Hey, Justice. What's up, boo?"

"Bitch, get over here now. I have to tell you something," Justice excitedly said into the phone.

"You can't tell me over the phone?"

"No, bitch, I have to show you."

"Ok, I'm on my way," Makyla finally said, agreeing to meet up with her best friend.

Makyla got off the phone then told April that she would be right back. She didn't plan on being gone that long because she wanted to be there when Bones walked in.

April gave her a hug. "You know what, Makyla, I love you and I'm more than happy to have you in me and my son's life. You and this baby is really a blessing to all of us."

Makyla tried not to cry, but her emotions got the best of her. "Thank you so much, and I love you too."

"Ok, you hurry up back so you can eat and rest for the rest of the day," April suggested right before Makyla walked out of the door.

Makyla hurried to find out what the emergency was with Justice.

Bones

Bones sat at the round table with Choppa and a few of their workers. It was time to bust a few niggas heads wide open behind Gunna's death.

"Big G, I heard you got some information for me. Go ahead, nigga, let it spill," Bones said, standing up.

"So, I talked to the guy at the gas station around the corner from his house. The young arab boy said he seen Gunna and Gina arguing with a nigga by the door. When me and Chase went up there, he showed us the video. You know Gunna was his nigga, so he was all for helping us."

Big G stood his fat ass up and gave Bones his phone. "See, Bones, I recorded it from the tape."

Bones watched the video before passing the phone around. He could see them arguing right before Mehki followed him away from the gas station. "Do any of you niggas recognize that nigga? Cause I sure don't."

Choppa looked at the video for the second time. "I know exactly who this nigga is. You know those spots we been running in? It's that nigga shit. He run that crew on the westside."

Everyone started looking at each other all crazy. They had been so busy playing bad asses that they never took the time to think about a nigga coming back for revenge. Now one of their own were dead behind a war that they started.

"What's this nigga info?" Bones then asked, breaking the silence.

Jim stood up. "His name is Mehki. I used to go to school with his little brother."

"So, where the fuck this nigga stay? I need him gone ASAP. This muthafucka killed my bro, and I don't feel comfortable knowing that he out here living his life like he ain't do shit wrong," Bones questioned.

Choppa dismissed everyone except for Big G.

"You know where that nigga stay at?" He asked.

"Yeah man, but I really don't wanna be in the middle of this shit. Like I said, I went to school with his brother and for the longest, I had the biggest crush on his baby sister. I think I gave y'all enough information."

"You a fat ass bitch. How the fuck did you ever make this team?" Bones said, pulling out his gun. "Now same question, different answer, you fat piece of shit."

Big G cried. He knew if he told what he knew or didn't tell, he was gonna end up dead in a field somewhere. Before Bones could pull the trigger, he quickly gave him the address.

Choppa shook his head at his homeboy. "Bro, you didn't have to kill that nigga. You knew he was gonna give up the info on that nigga."

"Yeah, the fuck I did. This nigga was a bitch and if push came to shove, this fat bitch was gonna run his fucking mouth to somebody. Y'all niggas worked with whoever raised their hand to make some money. I had to come home and get shit in order."

Choppa was tired of this nigga mouth and felt like it was time to put his ass in his place.

"See, bro, that's where you're wrong. You came out still on that bullshit from five years ago. We had everything under control, and everybody was eating. We didn't start having problems until you came up with the idea to go fuck with somebody else shit. Now Gunna dead behind that shit."

"So, what the fuck you sayin', nigga?" Bones barked.

"Nigga, you far from being stupid. You know exactly what the fuck I'm saying."

Both guys were heated at this point. Knowing exactly what he was trying to say, Bones lifted his gun up at his childhood friend. "You saying Gunna dead because of me? Cause if that's what you sayin' you can die right fucking now."

"Nigga, we grew up together and got the same attitude. Do what you gon' do ,my nigga. Fuck you and that gun, bro!" Choppa barked out before spitting on the floor.

"Fuck you, nigga," Bones said before walking out the house.

Any other nigga would have been dead by now, but Bones couldn't find it in his heart to kill Choppa. They had been friends since babies, and he always looked at that nigga like a brother. He was the only nigga alive that would ever get away with talking shit to him. Bones checked his feelings before driving off. He wanted to go take care of the nigga that killed his bro then head home to see Makyla. She had a way of making him feel better.

After all the bullshit that had went down, he was happy as fuck that his memory was good, and he was able to remember the address. He made it across to the other side of town in no time. As he parked up the street from Mehki's house, he waited and watched patiently. He couldn't wait to catch a nigga slipping. He thought to himself that this was the very reason nobody but Makyla and his mom knew where he rested his head and his mom's location wasn't in the hood around niggas. He wasn't making it easy for niggas to creep up on him.

He sat there holding his gun, thinking about leaving the game alone after this and moving away with Makyla. Although he had brought her a building for her store, they could easily sell it and buy a new one. He wondered if she would do it. This would have been the best time to see if she was really down for a nigga.

Justice

Mehki had just left to go pack his bags and Justice was waiting on Makyla to pull up. She couldn't wait to tell her the good news. Just as Justice was zipping up her luggage, she heard the doorbell going off. She knew right off that it was Makyla. Soon as she opened the door for her, she quickly threw her hand in Makyla's face.

"Bitch, I'm getting married."

"Oh my gawd! I'm so happy for you, boo!" Makyla yelled as they jumped up and down, full of excitement.

"Girl, Mehki proposed to me and we been locked up in this house fucking like rabbits. My mom has the baby again, so we about to go out of town and just do us for a week or so."

"Girl, you got that platinum pussy. Got a nigga like him on lock," Makyla teased.

"Yes, bitch. My baby really loves me."

"Hey, I know this is your moment, but I really wanna tell you something."

Justice could see that Makyla was serious now, so she took seat on the couch. "What's up, boo?"

Makyla took a seat right next to her friend. "So, I'm gonna have a baby," she slowly said.

"A baby, bitch? Are you serious? I'm gonna be an auntie?"

"Yes, yes, and yes. On top of that, today I found out that Mike's girlfriend, Roni, is also pregnant."

"Seriously, it seems like all of us are being rained on with nothing but blessings. I'm so happy for everyone," Justice said, rubbing Makyla's stomach.

"Whatever girl, I'm not even showing yet," Makyla said, laughing.

"Have you told Mehki yet?"

"Hell nah! Not yet, but I'm gonna go talk to him before you guys leave."

"I know how he can be at times, especially over you. So, do you want me to ride over to the house with you. You know I got your back, boo."

Makyla laughed, "Nah, I'm gonna take care of it on my own. That boy will be alright. But let me get out of here. I wanna stop by the house before I head back to Brandon's place."

"Ok, I'm gonna get back to packing and wait on your brother to get back here."

"Love you, boo."

"Girl, I love you too."

They gave each other a hug before Makyla walked out of the door. Justice hoped that Mehki didn't flip out 'cause he would have brought that bullshit back home and fucked up their getaway. Justice was happy for her friend and couldn't wait to be an auntie, but deep down inside, she wanted to tell Makyla how she really felt about her boo. She really didn't care too much for him. Just from

the first time that she met him, she could tell that he wasn't
shit.

Mehki, Bones, & Makyla

Mehki rushed home so he could pack for his get away with Justice. He had just dropped their son off for the week to his grandma and was ready to hit Vegas up. Rushing into his crib, Mehki never saw a nigga watching his every move. Bones quietly snuck on the porch. It was just his luck that Mehki didn't lock the door behind him. He drew his gun, waiting to put a bullet in his head.

Mehki walked into the living room carrying a bag with a few outfits. Looking up to a gun in his face startled him and he dropped the bag. "What the fuck?"

"Yeah, nigga, you made it too fucking easy to find your bitch ass!" Bones yelled.

"Man, what the fuck you want? Who the fuck are you?"

Bones tried to stay focused but a picture on the wall caught him off guard. Staring right at him was his baby, Makyla. He now was wondering what the fuck was really going on and how she knew this nigga.

Mehki could tell that Bones was no longer focused on him and took this time to charge at him. "Muthafucka!" He yelled.

Bones stupidly dropped his gun and the guys began to fight. Each went blow for blow, giving each other a run for their money. Bones gave Mehki a quick three piece that made him stumble. He then took that time to grab his gun. He pointed it back at Mehki and let one shot off in his chest. Mehki fell back on the floor in front of the TV. Because Bones gun had a silencer and Makyla's radio was loud, she never heard her brother get shot. Makyla had just walked in the front door and was met with a gun pointed right at her head.

"What the fuck, Brandon? What the fuck are you doing?" She yelled.

That's when she looked over to Mehki on the floor. As she rushed past Bones, she dropped to her knees crying.

"What the fuck did you do, Brandon? What the fuck did you do?"

"Makyla, what the fuck you doing here? How do you know this nigga?"

"He's my brother. Oh my gawd, why did you do this to him?" She yelled as she continued to cry.

Mehki tried to say something but could barely move. He knew he was a goner. All those years of being a thug in the street, and he fucked up by letting a nigga catch him slipping.

"It's ok, Mehki, it's gonna be ok," Makyla said, holding her brother on her lap.

Bones was confused at everything. How the fuck did he fall for the sister of his enemy. It only took him a few seconds before he concluded that everything had to end right then and there. Just as Mehki tried to grab his gun from under the TV stand, Bones shot him again. This time, straight in his head. Makyla jumped and screamed out in pain.

"No, Mehki! No, please don't leave me!" She cried out.

She tried to shake him, praying that he would get up, but it didn't work. Her big brother was gone. He lifted his gun back up.

"Please, baby. Please don't shoot me, Brandon," she begged.

It was hard to look her in the face as she begged for her life. Bones shook his head as he made the decision to end her life. He needed to leave and there was no way in the world that she could stay alive. Shit would never be the same.

"Brandon, I love you and I'm pre…"

Before she could finish her sentence, Bones let off a shot to match her brother's. "Sorry shit ain't work out for us."

Bones walked out of the house like nothing happened. He didn't feel bad because he told her from jump that he wasn't shit and she shouldn't waste her love on a nigga like him.

***

Twenty minutes later, Bones was pulling up to his crib. He never pictured having to kill Makyla, but shit happened every day. After killing her brother like that, she had to go too. Bones stepped into the living room and was surprised by the set up on the coffee table. He looked over the balloons, then the ultrasound picture. That's when it hit him what Makyla was trying to say before he killed her.

"Surprise, father to be!" April yelled out as she walked out of the kitchen and into the living room.

Bones felt like somebody had stabbed him in the heart as he fumbled back on the wall. His body then slid down to the floor. April had seen the look on her son after murdering someone and could tell that he had just handled his business. Only this time, he seemed to be bothered by the event. Bones clutched onto his chest and for the first time in years, he cried.

"What the fuck did you do, Bones?" She yelled.

He cried uncontrollable as he finally realized that he did love that girl and now her and his baby were gone all because of him and his pride. April saw how hurt her son was and knew that it only meant something bad had to have happened.

"What the fuck did you do, boy?" She yelled again as she pulled his hands from over his face.

"I thought I had to, ma. I really fucked up this time!" He cried out.

"What the fuck did you do muthafucka? What the fuck did you do?"

"I'm sorry, ma," was all he had to say for her to figure everything out.

April covered her mouth as she let out a scream. Her son had done some stupid shit in his lifetime, but she had to admit that this was the stupidest. She felt like her heart had been ripped out of her chest as she cried out for Makyla.

Mike
Two Months Later

Mike sat on the couch drinking his Hennessy straight out the bottle. Since the death of his brother and sister, he just hadn't been the same. He had slowly become an alcoholic and it was killing him every single day that he couldn't find the nigga that killed them.

Roni walked into the living room rubbing her round belly. "Baby, you coming to bed or what?"

"Nah, but you can go ahead and go to bed."

"Mike, baby. I know you're still hurting, but you have to get some rest. You've been up just drinking and shit, that's not healthy."

Mike was now irritated by her. He had his moments when he just wanted to be left alone and now was that time. He loved her but he wasn't in the mood to hear about what he should and shouldn't be doing.

"Look, go ahead and get in the bed. I'm about to go to the store right quick and I'll be back. Do you want something back?"

"Some sunflower seeds and a pickle," she said with a smile on her face.

Mike gave her a kiss before walking out the door. He really just needed some fresh air before he ended up going off on Roni for no fucking reason. At the end of the day, he knew she only was looking out for him.

After grabbing Roni's snacks, he started to walk back to his car. He usually didn't pay muthafuckas any attention, but it was a face that stood out. He now was rocking a low haircut, but it was the same nigga. Mike thought back to the day him and Justice were talking, and she showed him a picture of Bones that she had snuck and took when they had gone to the club one night. She had explained how he always rubbed her the wrong way although she was only around him that one time. Word had got back to him that Makyla was fucking with this nigga on the other side of town, and he was responsible for killing Mehki and Makyla. When he didn't show up to her funeral, he knew that it had to be true. Mike opened the glovebox and pulled out his gun. It was time for this nigga to pay for his pain. As Bones opened the car door, Mike stepped right back out of his car. Aiming his gun straight at Bones, he didn't give a fuck who was around.

POW! POW! POW!

Bones never knew what hit him as his body hit the ground. That bitch Karma had finally come to collect from his ass.

The End

Let's have a one on one book discussion. You can email me at <u>Messiah.nf@gmail.com</u>.

Do you think Makyla played herself by constantly telling Bones that she loved him although he never said it back?

Were you surprised that Mehki took Justice back after her sex tape was sent to him?

What do you think will happen with Mike and Roni now?

Who was your favorite character?

Who was your least favorite character?

What did you think about April?

Did you think Bones really loved Makyla?

After killing Mehki, did you think that it was only right that Bones killed Makyla? Did you feel like his reason was legit?

Did you feel bad about Rell getting killed?

If Bones never had got killed do you think that April could ever forgive her son?

If you have any of your own questions, please don't be afraid to ask me.

Book Catalog

Intrigued by a Savage Love

Finding Love in a Real Boss 1 & 2

Nasir and Kennedy: A Luv from the Gutta

In Love with a Street Princess

To Be Loved by a Brick Boy 1, 2, & 3

When Love Calls the Shots

All cried Out: Loving a Detroit Nigga 1&2

Contact Information

Follow me on Facebook: Author T Friday

Follow me on Instagram: Authortfriday

I'm also on Twitter: @FridayAuthor

If you haven't already sign up for my email blast for new updates on all my books. Messiah.NF@Gmail.com